INROADS

Stories

William Auten

FIRE IN HAND MEDIA

ISBN (print): 9780578866581
ISBN (ebook): 9798986092706

Published by Fire in Hand Media
Fire In Hand Media colophon is a registered trademark of Fire In Hand Media LLC
fireinhand.com

CONTENTS

Bloodsuckers 3

King Tide 18

Cardinal 26

Home Improvement 46

Names of Horses 50

Strike Sides 59

Dioramas 81

Inroads 85

All Clear 106

Creek on the Right 123

Moonflowers 128

Skeleton Key 143

Clean Slate 148

Like Land Does 169

Body Bearers 185

INROADS

Stories

Bloodsuckers

Mosquitoes cling to the father and son as they slog to the barn through humidity; buckets, brooms, and mops thump their thighs and hips. Cutting across greens sealing the front and back yards, they sop puddles on the grill, chairs, and table and around the foundation and near Lisa's garden.

Matt points to the gutter snaking through the yard. Ben grabs a garbage bag, rakes debris blocking rainwater, and when he holds up a wet clump, he resembles a cub on his hind legs. Matt sloshes over, and he and Ben chuckle at the county's flier: NOTICE TO DRAIN STANDING WATER – MOSQUITOES CARRY DISEASES – FAILURE TO DO SO WITHIN THIRTY DAYS WILL RESULT IN FINES. When Matt and Lisa read it, they threw up their hands as more rain rolled in and soaked their ankle-high grass, their outdoor furniture and property's low points, and their neighbors' yards.

Matt checks Ben when he wheezes and tugs his sweat-darkened hoodie, and after the boy confirms he's OK, Matt stuffs the flier in his pocket and slaps himself in the grass glowing like dollar bills.

They work their way down the backyard and more than halfway to the barn where Matt says, "Your mom said you've been in front of the mirror more. Let me take a look."

Ben juts his fuzzy chin and upper lip.

"I didn't shave until I was about fifteen. Your grandad showed me with a safety razor. That blade can slice you up real good if you don't pay attention. These bugs will be all over you in a heartbeat." Matt's gloves scamper along his neck miming blood dripping down. "Thought about anything special you want at your party? Those ice cream sandwiches from Piggly Wiggly?"

"Only if we can have the green mint, not the red."

"They upset your stomach last time, didn't they?"

Ben nods.

"Maybe you ate them too fast. They were pretty good."

"Yeah. At first."

"Listen…about that camp you want this summer. Your mom and I would like for you to go, but if we can't, is there something else you want?"

"No. Well…a computer would be nice because I could code whenever I want. And, if it were a laptop, I could take it wherever, and I wouldn't have to go to the camp."

Matt grimaces. "Your mom and I would get you that if we could, and we want to, but a promise is the best we can give right now."

"I can just move to Silicon Valley when I'm old enough."

"Do you how much it is to live there?"

Ben shrugs.

"Come on. Let's check the Four-Zero."

BLOODSUCKERS

The rusted lock clicks off, the barn doors open, and hot moisture billows out. Matt pushes back his ball cap. Winches, tools, sawdust soaking oil spots, and fiberglass clippings litter the broken-up floor. Water drops from the ceiling and slides off grease-smeared wood and metal. Mosquitoes float like puppets on strings around the blue tarp covering the stock car Matt bought, hoping it would be a father-son project and would supplement income after he lost his job at the plant and pawned jewelry, electronics, and guns—anything to help while Lisa picked up more hours at the hospital. But the spreadsheet of winnings and expenses built by Ben and Matt's plan of drive hard and fast until greenbacks overflowed remain in the red. Lisa reminds him that providing for a family isn't about things: "We love you, no matter what. Don't do anything desperate. Let's be patient." He has repeated something similar to Ben and Kendra, telling them to focus on church, family, school, and being a good person, but by the time those words reach them, they drift asleep, and when they wake, Matt bears the weight of them in a new day.

The blue tarp settles along the tires, and the Forty sits in morning light and workshop lamps. Matt leans over the scuffs and dents in the middle of the right-side door near the decal of Quick Copy & Printing that swapped advertising space for fuel before it ran out of business. On winter days, Matt fired the engine, which boomed as though God charged a cavalry through the bare oaks.

Ben pulls his hoodie off his swollen face. "What time's the race?"

"High noon. And I promise I will be done in time for your party. After a victory lap and my picture with the mayor."

"I hope you win something."

"Me too."

"Kendra wouldn't mind. She's been talking about her recital outfit."

"Yeah, that's important to her." Matt drags a mop over the tarp. "If you had a computer, I bet you could figure out faster laps, smoother aerodynamics. Maybe run some tests."

"You wouldn't lose. They'd all think you're cheating."

Matt stops himself from mentioning a website Ben could build after Matt schemed one night about stealing his rivals' parts and selling them online "because they win all the time, and I don't know how they do it or how to stop them." Lisa begged Matt not to bring Ben into that—or for him to lose himself in that. Turning over in bed, Matt assured her neither he nor Ben would do that: "The Devil landed on my shoulder and whispered it." He stares at the Forty before staring outside. The path he and Ben trampled bends and winds into the barn and, blending into patches of concrete and grass, spreads under the stock car like wings. Matt swats and wipes himself. "Bloodsuckers everywhere," he mutters.

. . .

Matt stops in front of a photograph of Wilky and his dad holding beer cans and a wreath race officials and the CEO of a frozen-chicken company awarded them. Under two checkered flags tacked to the garage's main wall glistens a check from last season; zeroes after the dollar sign and first number dot the long line. Sunlight pours in under the half-raised door and highlights awards, trophies, and stickers of manufacturers slapped on cabinets and toolboxes; a newspaper article of the big man winning three weekends in a row; and, sealed behind glass, the first dollar Wilky won.

"There's some coffee, if you want." The big man steps into the garage, closes the door to the house, and gestures toward the carafe on the counter and its sink, towel dispenser, and an eyewash station. He yanks a chair after swatting mosquitoes.

Matt looks around and turns over a bucket.

"So, what's up? You want to talk strategy for the race? Finally ready for some pointers?" Wilky's smirk, with his never-stained dentures after a five-car wreck nearly ended his career, grows inside his beard.

"Ben's birthday is coming up. He'll be thirteen. Old as your boy."

"When's the big day?"

"Saturday."

"Same day as the race.

"Yep. He wants a computer. He's into that."

"Kyle's seen him in that after-school class. He thought maybe Ben was in detention." The big man chuckles. "He's a smart kid. Yours, not mine."

"I want to ask a favor from you." Matt shifts on the bucket. "I want to win Saturday's race."

"You serious?" Wilky's laughter echoes in the garage. "Oh, hell, you are."

"I could use the money."

"We all could use the money. Times are tough for everybody. But I ain't no charity. All this is earned, not given. Besides, I got my own to look out for. I got four mouths to feed. Sara telecommuting to Danville. And now her parents are starting to decline."

"Would you be willing to let me lead enough to earn the laps-led bonus? That's it. It's not much money."

"Any money's good money. And that bonus is good money."

"It's not the whole pot."

"That don't matter."

"It won't even cover the cost of Ben's present. Just some of it." He leans closer to Wilky. "You should see him with that stuff. He has a gift. He's not an athlete. This is his thing. We just want to see him right by it."

"A computer?"

"Or this computer camp he wants to go to. Both. Either."

Wilky swirls his mug. "They'll be other birthdays. His eighteenth before he says goodbye to this place and heads off to college. On his sixteenth give him the Forty, unless your daughter wants it."

"Just those laps. That's it. You can win the whole thing. We can even agree who gets which laps. You and I can switch. We can talk about that right here and now." Matt jabs at the floor. "I can drift back, after I've cemented my spot, fake a bad engine."

"You've thought this through, haven't you?" The big man's flannelled chest rises and sinks. He detangles his beard; silver and black hairs glide among the breeze and mosquitoes. "You're not winning that race. I can tell you that for sure."

Matt gnaws his bottom lip. "What about those laps?"

"Just those laps?"

"Yeah."

"Then what?"

"You do what you're best at. You win. Go home with another notch in your legend. The Jasper Jet."

The big man crosses his ankles; the heels of his shoes thump concrete; his dark eyes lock on Matt. "I'll let you know."

"When?"

"Well, hell, Matt, I didn't know you were in such a hurry." The chair creaks when he pushes out. "I got to go see my dad."

"How's he doing?"

"I think the prognosis won't be what we want."

"I'm sorry to hear that. Tell him I said hi."

"I'll do that. Thank you."

"Let me know about the race."

"Close the garage door on your way out. Button's over there." Wilky's scarred, bloated fingers point to a control panel near the refrigerator. "It'll lock on its own. Tell your kids and Lisa hi."

The sound of Wilky's truck dissipates down the road. Matt surveys the area, believing he's alone. Wilky's closest neighbors live acres away in a farmhouse tucked inside a grove that, on Matt's drive over, the downpours had thickened. One night, when Wilky and Sara invited over friends, families, and supporters of racers, Matt stood inside that grove and, under the stars, talked to Hoyt Sr. who had fought his first battle with lung cancer after years of working in the mines. He told Matt to live far below his means because no political party could sustain its promises and because chasing life through fog and across rocks and alongside cliffs is the only chase before life drains itself dry.

Matt pushes a different button, and the door dividing the garage and workshop opens, segment by segment, where Wilky's Twelve gleams under rows of lights clicking on. Matt double-checks outside—wind and puddles on the road. His boots nearly scuff the new tires as he steps closer; he steps away, glances behind him, steps closer. He grips one of the clips holding down the Twelve's hood, looping his finger through it like a grenade pin. His quick tug of the first one, and then the rest exposes the engine. Matt walks into the workshop, scans outside and the house, and from a cabinet, grabs pliers. He swats away mosquitoes and, alongside the Twelve, finds a part Wilky and pre-race inspection should ignore. Drenched in sweat, he twists and bends until the pliers bite.

. . .

An official climbs into the tower overlooking the track and readies the green flag. The cars kill their engines for the national anthem. Matt peers over at trailers, vehicles, and the stalls and pits before returning to Tyrese's voice quivering as she finishes, lowers the microphone, and wipes mascara; the crowd erupts. Matt smiles at the young woman he's known since she was a toddler and who Lisa babysat when Tyrese's mother took the late-night shift at a truck stop that closed only for Christmas. After the mortgage and bills flooded the family, Tyrese's dad shot himself. "Honey, I'm so sorry," Matt whispered to Kendra who pleaded with him never to do that. He watches the areas leading to the track entrance and chews the inside of his cheek—no more racers roll in. Before sliding on his helmet, he spits red on the track.

The grandstand speakers squawk *Gentlemen, start your engines!*

The cars rumble alive; exhaust and noise thicken the humid afternoon. The sun has warmed the track for hours. Mosquitos congregate near water fountains and the concession stand. Matt fidgets. In the distance, a driver, the track's smoke and heat blurring his stout body, straddles the concrete barrier, one leg at a time, and lumbers to his car. An official stops the late driver before letting him continue.

Matt jolts forward but recedes when he sees the colors of the driver's suit. "Hey, Tim!"

"Yo, Matt, what's up?"

"Have you seen Wilky?"

"He's at the hospital. His dad's cancer's back big time. Terminal. Maybe one month left." Tim straps his helmet, clicks his steering wheel in place, and revs his engine.

The green flag drops, and during the race's first half, Matt neither fights for the lead, finds himself in the top ten, nor rests in the bottom. He drifts among the bloated middle. The Three wiggled free, and Matt had a chance, but it slipped away as quickly as it appeared. He could drive backward, and the scene would be the same.

The unbroken mass buzzes around the track and lulls the crowd's roar. The last-lap flag will soon drop, and Matt has to move as though competition is invisible. He could draft behind a car to pull his way to the front, weaving in and out of traffic, or be content with a lukewarm result but a safe return home to Lisa's prayers that he survives his races; to Kendra's joy that her dad is, as her Father's Day gift to him said on the t-shirt, WORLD'S GREATEST DAD; and to Ben's birthday party. He could push for a better finish at the next race; he could travel to races in other counties or nearby states; he could set aside time for more practice, which will be impossible because of the schedules Lisa and he agreed on after arguing about priorities and money. Before he left for today's race, he kissed Lisa and the kids goodbye. "Don't be late for us," she said, hanging birthday streamers on the back porch and barn. Had Wilky been here, Matt could have clawed to the front, dueled with the Jasper Jet for the number one spot, and had his name rung from the speakers: *Ladies and gentlemen, Matthew Reece is our Laps-Led Winner! First time this season. He'll receive a nice check, thanks to ChemRight Fertilizer.* But Matt's foot eases off the accelerator, and he drifts from fourteenth to last to taking the pit road, floating like a bug downstream. *The Forty might be experiencing a mechanical problem.*

Matt pushes through the window's safety net and waves to the crowd before they cheer louder for the reduced field thundering for the finish. He pulls into the stall where he waited for Wilky, loads the Forty onto the trailer, and rumbles off while, behind him, the race rushes on.

• • •

After pulling into the parking lot, Matt runs to the second-floor desk where he spots Lisa. "Hey, hon…hon," he says, panting.

"I thought I was supposed to meet you at home. My shift's not done." Lisa checks the clock and then Matt's race attire. "What did you do?"

"Where's Hoyt Wilkinson's room?"

She types on the computer and tells him the number.

"Man, you did get done early." Wilky flashes race updates as they roll across his phone. "There's about seventeen laps left. Beyner is going to win, unless he loses a tire, which could happen because he knows his palm in a bathroom better than the grooves. He'll learn the hard way."

"I damaged your Twelve." Matt wipes his face.

"I know. Dad got real bad before anything you did made it worse."

The breathing-machine between the men chirps; blood drips from the IV bag into a tube pinched in Hoyt Sr.'s arm.

"Is that your vehicle out there?"

Matt spins toward the other man's voice in the doorway. "Hey, D.J."

The policeman demurs.

"Officer Timmins, sir."

The short officer, writing in his log book, throws his bald head toward to the window. "That's yours, right?"

Matt peers through the blinds. Two squad cars surround his Forty, trailer, and truck. "Yes, it is."

"You parked in an area designated for hospital employees. And you parked in a haphazard manner." Officer Timmins messages to his shoulder radio. "Were you at Mr. Wilkerson Jr.'s property the afternoon of the ninth?"

"I was."

"Do you know anything about damage to his vehicle?" He flips through his log book. "The engine. A stock car he uses for racing."

Matt glances at Wilky holding his dad's hand. "I do."

The big man's knees creak when he stands up. "D.J., come on out here for a sec."

The door closes after Wilky and Officer Timmins. The room flows through Matt as he sits with Hoyt Sr. Matt and his sisters stood in a similar room in the same hospital after their mother's heart attack rendered her unconscious. She had named her oldest child her executor, responsible for her end-of-life directive, which Matt knew about but never considered because, when Stacey emailed a copy, his mother's decision was as distant as the next season of rain. On a couch in a waiting area down the hall, Lisa cradled the kids as Kendra stroked Ben's head and whispered, "It's OK, Benny. Gamma is in Heaven with Gampa." Matt and Lisa wanted the kids to be present, but Ben shook like something bit him. Matt sniffles as he sits next to Hoyt Sr. settling in the bed like when a body is ready.

Officer Timmins steps back into the room. "Mr. Wilkerson will not be pressing charges regarding his vehicle, but you need to move yours now."

Lisa knocks on the door. "Just stopping by to see how everyone is doing before I leave work."

"Wilky, I…"

The big man's hand smothers Matt's words. "Don't you have somewhere you need to be?"

. . .

Friends, family, and neighbors sing "Happy Birthday" as they circle Ben who squints and jitters in place through the last verse and then mumbles a thanks to everyone, reaches for his headphones, and slides behind his sister as she hugs him and gives him a book on World War II codebreakers and repair manuals for small electronics—FROM ALL OF US the card said. The circle breaks for bowls of chips and dips; plates of grilled meats and veggies; and soft drinks, beer, and ice-cream sandwiches stuffed in coolers. The Forty shines as the sunset flows across the open barn doors.

Matt dares the cousins to fold a slice of pepperoni pizza around an ice-cream sandwich.

"That's gross, Uncle Matt. But we dare you to do it."

He gags but swallows the mixture before nausea sucks color from him. He sticks out his green tongue when he walks past the adults who offer a shot of whiskey. The kids scream and giggle when one of the boy cousins attempts to down one slice of supreme between two ice-cream sandwiches. A roll of paper towels and a garbage bag appear next to him.

Linking her arm in Matt's and kissing him, Lisa whispers, "What time are you headed to Wilky's tomorrow?"

"After breakfast."

The oncoming night lifts the day's heat. Kendra whirls her skirt through the air; she repeats a phrase from French class about summer moons. Ben wanders off with cousins when they spot something glowing near tall grass and oaks in the corner by the barn.

"Justin Trumwell called Kendra the other day."

"Maybe Ben can build an app for tracking her. And Justin Trumwell."

"The fun's just beginning." Lisa brightens in the citronella candles shooing away mosquitoes. "For everybody."

Matt walks toward the tall grass and oaks, calls Ben over, wraps his arm around him, and asks if he'd like to help with a project—an intricate repair—that could use his attention. And he tells him the money isn't around this year but they have time, as they stand between the backyard and the barn and lightning bugs moving in the grass.

King Tide

At the top of the stairs, I yell at Keith we have to hurry and go now because the time has changed. My heart races. My head throbs. I can't tie my shoes faster. His shoes clack on the tile, and the liquor cabinet clangs. I yell again while he probably downs a shot before we leave. His cologne enters our bedroom before he does. Loosening his tie, he asks what's going on, and I throw my head toward the television. "They've upped it by fifteen minutes." My legs shiver from being in bed all day. I had waited for him to wake me until it was time for us to see Cody.

Keith slips on his tattered and sweat-stained runners that have stunk up our closet since he began running a loop every morning to the ocean and back home. My husband the novice athlete. He's been talking about changing that route—something more straight-forward, out and back on a line, avoiding the beach, water, and everything in the sunrise and shadows, saying it's time for that kind of change. I fumble for my jacket while reaching for the bannister. I've yet to return to the gym or my knitting group.

The ticker at the bottom of the evening news lists the streets the King Tide will affect when it reaches land. Cameras switch to crews laying sandbags alongside amateur meteorologists ready to record the ocean breaching dikes, jetties, and seawalls. A map's blue ovals predict coastal and inland flooding. Three years ago, we saw what had been the usual spot for high tide—soft sand, foam bubbling in our tracks, buildings and sidewalks too far away. Cody loved everything at the beach. Our only child was a child of the water. We told him he was born under the spell of a high-tide full moon, which was so powerful that it, so badly wanting him to be in our arms, pulled him out of me early. He had magical powers, we winked at him, especially when he clipped a black-and-white checkered towel around his neck and proclaimed that one day he would balance the world on his shoulders so that no one would spill out and be alone.

On the kitchen counter I set a box of juice that, every time he drank it, stained his lips. We teased him about all those women at temple kissing him because, with his round cheeks and red curls, he was irresistible.

Keith removes his glasses and rubs his eyes. "Ready?" He muffles the car keys.

I grab a pen and the blank card for Cody before we drive from the lights lining our neighborhood that tightens inside the cool night and, their windows glowing with neighbors who have stopped asking about us and offering help.

I finish writing our note in my lap. "Can you go faster? It'll be underwater."

"I'm doing the best I can." Keith has not moved his hand off the steering wheel and onto my knee like he has when we drove here in the past. He hasn't looked at me. He stares ahead as though he's plowing into an unknown that has no power over him.

Traffic waxes and wanes on our way to the boardwalk. An ambulance rushes toward residential areas, not the beach. The blue and red lights of patrol cars burst in our empty backseat. Cody would stutter "Po-po-po-lice" whenever he saw one and sounded like a kid who heard rap for the first time. Ms. Alison, his speech therapist from second to fifth grade helped him improve. His R's no longer sounded like a motor skipping in neutral. "Cody Code-Man from the VAB!" we'd riff to a beat Keith tapped on the dashboard while he drove us to his parents' place in West Chester or to New Jersey for mine. Cody would fall asleep in the backseat by the time we reached Richmond, if we took the western route, or when we crossed into Delaware. He always held a juice box I'd gently take from him when he twitched with dreams.

Pedestrians come and go like it's any night on the main strip. The lights in the rooms of The James and other hotels are as full and bright as during summers and holidays—so many guests staying put. The radio says highways are starting to back up and the water shouldn't rise much past Chesapeake Street where stores along the beach will get the brunt of the flooding. Shadows walking on the sidewalks dump large sandbags in front of windows, driveways, and doors. Other shadows sit in lawn chairs on roofs. Some of them are grilling and raising glasses and bottles.

When a detour takes us too far north, we wind inland through blocks of offices, shops, and restaurants that limit views of the ocean. A helicopter over us disappears. Keith exits near Old Dominion Donuts. Tourists have ignored caution tape surrounding the statue of Neptune, perched on the beach, gripping his triton and flanked by creatures and waves— everything frozen in time. A club's outdoor heat lamps flame out, and under neon-purple lights, groups of people cradling drinks shuffle inside. We reach the last third of the road. Black water rumbles up the shore.

After the first year Cody was gone, we debated how best to remember him. Where he was last seen? On his birthday? Keith's side urged for the latter, saying the parade and fireworks on the day we lost Cody were too joyous for our family's loss— "wouldn't feel right," Bubbie Esther said. My father said we should do something every day every month until Cody returned, which he prayed wouldn't be the case, even something as small as singing his favorite songs. "Send us pictures of his drawings on Mondays, pictures of him on Fridays!" Dad cried. On the seventh of October, we drive down here, as we have for the past three years, for Cody's birthday and where he was last seen. Tonight, with the King Tide crashing harder against the pier, he turns twelve.

Keith pulls the car over.

"What are you doing?"

"The water takes away everything we put there." He chokes before speaking again. "And if not, the beach bums do."

"You don't know that."

"You don't either."

I stare out the window. "The water isn't like last year."

"That doesn't matter."

"That's not the point."

"He's not coming back."

"You're wrong." I roll down my window. The moon sparkles on the black ocean. The waves churn louder. "And you'll regret being wrong."

"They've had three years for new clues, new leads. Nothing."

"Clues can take a long time to show up. A decade maybe."

"No new witnesses. No bad guys ratting out other bad guys. Nothing else like this has happened in the region. Copycat crimes or some pattern."

"They'll be found. They'll make a mistake."

"If it's really a 'them.' You know how many curly-haired boys wearing a baseball cap were down there that day? The Neville triplets wore the same hats so Jim and Margaret would see them. I waved to them getting sno-cones."

A motorcycle drifts by. A girl clings to the driver and holds a selfie stick. They turn for the parking lot under floodlights and glowing vests. The radio reminds us what we're about to experience is natural, expected, but not an everyday occurrence.

Cool air rushes in as Keith rolls down his window. "Marques told me he could be pulled off our case. He said he had a new case, and with ours not moving, they'll probably pull him. We would remain 'open.' Not closed but not moving."

"When did he tell you this?"

"The other night he stopped by."

"He stopped by?"

Keith leans back in his seat. "They're limited with their help. He offered other options."

"Cases can be connected. They need us. Cody is still out there."

"Something would have broken open by now. He's not coming back."

I stumble out of the car, slamming the door. Waves rumble closer to the shore. Cars honk and sirens echo somewhere in the dark. Keith calls out as he jogs after me. I walk to the point on the pier where we don't know if it's where Cody was taken, but the water and the moonlight have yet to tell me otherwise. Few people are here. Keith has stopped running, and closer behind me, he breathes heavier, faster. He ran into the crowds overwhelming the beach and yelled for Cody that day, the sun brightened everything, and I could only see figures moving like flames and the ocean flickering like the white-hot center. A circle of men and women yelled and searched with Keith and then, when noon turned to sunset, comforted us until police said we should reorganize at the station.

We believe he might have been taken by friendly strangers, maybe a couple who wanted a child of their own—this theory investigators have stitched together for us. Someone saw a woman kneel in front of a ginger boy who was lost and crying near Atlantic Bike Rental. The man with her—maybe a dark goatee, maybe tattoos, maybe clean shaven and no tattoos, looking "like a normal nice guy"—told people they were the boy's friends and would take him to his parents.

Our plan that weekend was to be down at the beach all day and stay for the fireworks at night. The Fourth of July here always bursts with noise and pageantry. Summer is in full swing by then, tourists and locals spill onto every street, and Revolutionary War actors fill the parade between beach and city. The news meteorologist at the time assured us the tropical storm would not strengthen into a hurricane and land here. So many balloons floated off wrists in the hot air. Cody slipped from us, and he walked ahead of us, trying to get one. We let him. His Phillies hat bobbed in the afternoon light and among the smells of hot dogs, nachos, pizza, and sunscreen—and then disappeared as quickly as the crowd's laughter and chatter smothered us.

On the pier, I tape our note to the box of fruit juice. I have not stopped asking God what is to be done with the years that have yet to stop sinking. "Thy will…" Rabbi's words ring in my head. The water splashes over the pier, seeps through the bottom. The wood creaks underneath me. My soles are wet. I turn around. I am the only one here. The tide will erase the shore, where the shadow of Keith retreats a little more each time the water rolls closer to the mainland. I step back into a darkness that neither rises nor falls, is not seen but is felt, and covers the ground until it is too dark to sleep.

Cardinal

The bird drops like blood on a branch before bounding toward the fire escape where Winny smothers his cigarette in water seeping through ice the late afternoon melts. He fishes for a pouch and a book atop his nightstand inside the window. Spreading its wings but staying put, the cardinal chirps, strikes its small flame of a beak on concrete and trash, and spikes seeds Winny tossed. It glides toward the ledge dividing traffic, offices, condos, and public housing from the blue sky it breaks red when it flies away.

At the back of his book, Winny darkens a circle on dog-eared pages he blocked like a calendar and records the cardinal. His marks rest between the book's illustrations, descriptions, ranges, mating habits, diets, and songs. Pictures of newborn cardinal chicks are as pink as the flecks of scars between his knuckles and crooks of his elbows.

After the cardinal lands on the rooftop across from his room, Winny adds an arc—dates and times or squiggled clock-face hands scribbled under each arc—curving down like flight paths onto his drawing of the rooftop and its trees, umbrellas and chairs, a bar that serves drinks to crowds, and a waterfall that bounds over the bricks but never touches the street. His finger trails under a sentence until his mouth spins; he stumbles on the

Latin and descriptions, starts again, stutters, and, grimacing, closes the book. The ABCs, numbers under one hundred, everyday symbols, such as dollars and cents, and writing his full name, birthdate, address at the rehab center, and Social Security number no longer trouble him. The day Russ explained punctuation, Winny traced a question mark in red under his sketch of the rooftop.

Sunlight spreads further across the squat all-glass buildings surrounding Winny. He brushes his stringy hair, runs his tongue over remaining teeth, winces after splashing too much cologne on his collar, and rummages in his closet. Ketchup stains his other button-down, and the second-hand store managed by the rehab center closes soon. His tie and plaid vest cover his shirt wrinkles, and he hooks a silver four-leaf clover on a loose button. Into his backpack he drops a water bottle, a snack bar, the bird book and a pen rubber-banded across the cover, and a large-font email. His phone alarm chimes: YOU INTERVIEW 1 HOUR.

Stopping at a room on his way out, he asks, "How'd it go?"

The woman takes off her headphones. "My mouth ran way out in front of me once again. Like a bat out of hell." She fidgets with her purple-tipped hair. "'Tell us about your experience.' 'Well, at thirty-seven and with that super-gappy resume in front of you, I'll probably be your extra-special-learning-curve project.'" Makenzay shifts on the bed. "'Where do you see yourself in five years?' I laughed out loud at that one.

They laughed too but in that awkward let's-move-on kind of way. Cool, you know? Whatever. And then this nugget. 'How would you handle confrontation in our office?' I saw myself flipping off my ex. But I did it in my head, unlike other times." She pats her back while giving a thumbs-up.

"That's progress."

"But then I said, 'Oh…' And that was it. Not even some b.s. like, 'HR is often under-appreciated and a misunderstood team member, and I'd value their blah, blah, blah.' I came in with this new image Russ gave them, but I had nothing to back it up." Music fades from her headphones. "I just want someone to take a chance on me."

"I got the Hyatt today. Room service at your service."

"Damn. Look at you. Good luck." Makenzay slides on her headphones, dabs her eyeliner, and waves to Winny's "Thanks. See ya."

Before signing out downstairs, Winny knocks on an office door.

"Hey there." Russ stops typing on his computer. "You off?"

"Yes, sir."

"Got any questions or concerns?"

"Anything else you can give me?"

"This one's all you. Go get it." The big man pumps his clasped hands. "And when you're done, we're looking forward to hearing from you tonight."

"See you at seven."

Winny crosses the street, lunch-hour traffic honking and squealing, and coats and jackets congesting sidewalks. In the middle of a row of shops, he turns under the shoe-repair sign and the art gallery's repeating film of protestors, linked arm-in-arm and tied by signs, marching toward but never reaching the athletes on posters and neon beers of the sports bar next door; he turns again, blocks down where the cartoon chicken sits on waffles, before heading toward burned-down row houses, the former home of a tobacco company transformed into tech incubators, and the graffitied bus stop where asterisks scroll across the ticker before the new estimated arrival for Winny's bus flashes. Two women sitting on the bench grumble about the delay and hail a taxi.

He compares the numbers on his phone's clock and alarm to the ticker's update: twenty-three minutes past the scheduled time. His left middle finger pushes on his location on the bus stop's map and, stepping back to double-check the order of streets he practiced last week, spins his forefinger down to the block curving with the land that follows an elbow of the river and, far southwest of him, ends at the Hyatt. Freezing his left fingers, his right hand pulls up Russ's office address; he runs the numbers and letters atop the stop's map until they match an advertisement over a fast-food restaurant he and Makenzay have been to. Phone under his chin, Winny measures his walk to the bus stop from the center's front door—from the tip of his fingernail he cleaned and clipped extra short, after Russ told him about the interview, to the faded blue tattoo of the date, between his joints and knuckles, when his girlfriend overdosed and he could not read the numbers to dial 9-1-1. The V of his left hand extends to his right: where he came from is longer than where he has to be.

Wind gouges the warmth inside the stop as Winny's alarm sounds: YOU INTERVIEW THIRTY MINUTES. He scratches his legs as his knees pump; he devours half his snack bar and guzzles his water. A man sitting upright against a boarded-up storefront snores himself awake; his dog yips as Winny approaches but then quiets when he offers a bite. Winny takes his time copying Russ's contact information onto a blank page in his book, scribbles out missteps—the writing less like a child's than it used to be—and wipes his water bottle's mouth. He gives all that plus the rest of his snack bar to the man. Rideshares and cyclists weave through the streets. Foot and automobile traffic thicken. Another taxi putters by, idles, moves on. Winny remeasures the space on the map from the bus stop to the hotel and checks his phone's clock. Church bells announce quarter-till. He tightens his stocking cap and walks briskly, deeper through areas of the city where promises of new beginnings remain grounded.

When his last alarm sounds, his pace quickens along the canals threading through the financial district and toward the hotel. The river, on the other side of the flood wall, rushes over rocks and around pillars that held train tracks. Tucked inside crumbling bricks and mortar and under rebar and vines, one pillar holds a nest and a camera Russ told Winny about.

"She's got babies," Russ said. "You can watch them online."

"I know, but they're just ospreys."

"You got your favorites now?" Russ chuckled.

"Ever seen a cardinal in snow?"

The big man shook his head no.

"Ever cut yourself and soak it up with toilet paper?"

"Shaving."

"They don't always leave for winter."

"Did you read about that?"

"I worked on the word *migrate* one day." Winny shied away. "I was supposed to work on my math homework."

"That's OK."

"My book's got all these pictures, but when I could spell 'cardinal,' I found more on the web."

"Good."

"At this one site you can list all the times you see one. They have a map you can click. And this movie had them flying real slow so you could see their wings spread out. Like running your fingers through red dirt."

As Winny turns on a corner reserved for condos and shops, the hotel emerges behind the flood wall. He reckons the ospreys and nest are gone: maybe the weather or another bird occupies the spot—the babies nudged onto their wings.

"Good afternoon." The front-desk attendant smiles. "How may I help you?"

Winny slides the email her way. "I have a job interview."

The attendant places a call and points down a hall—third door on the right highlighted by a photographer's exhibition.

Before entering the room, Winny stops at a water fountain, but it doesn't relieve him.

"Winston Lang?" A man peers over papers while sitting at the table.

"Yes, sir." Winny glances at the email. "Mister…Ru-iz."

"You're late. I don't interview people who are tardy."

"The bus never showed up. I walked here."

"I appreciate that."

Winny wipes his brow and smoothes his vest; his stuttering increases. "I can work late night or early. I'll take another route my first day. The center can drop me off."

"I have a four-thirty on the way. Thank you for stopping by." Mr. Ruiz motions toward the door opposite a wall and its photo of trees, spring colors, the gold of low sunlight, and in the middle of the road leading to an old country church, deer caught between being left behind, moving without being noticed, and catching up to their family's far-ahead silhouettes.

Winny starts back for the center but turns for the pedestrian bridge suspended under the interstate. Cars and semis thunder over him and rattle cables; echoes head to terminals split in opposite directions from where Winny stands at the guardrail. Runners pushing strollers pass him. A man in a suit and loose tie lights a joint. Sparrows circle a brace before nesting in shadows, and on the back of the email, Winny sketches them and the structure hiding them until a great blue heron lands in the marshes where it stabs but fishes back nothing and then splashes in the spot brackish from the churn of the James River and the Atlantic. Winny repeats the shape of the bird's neck until the lines of S's evolve into roads without beginnings or ends.

Around a crook of the river, halfway between the city's shoreline and the island's forests and ghosts of Powhatans, slaves, and soldiers, kayakers roll in rapids brightened by patches of snow. The slim hulls—one lava red; the other sky blue—curl, dip, and return to the surface. Winny looks down the crook and sees new blocks of development and, under it, remains of the mobile-home park where he lived with his aunt and uncle.

"You don't want to or can't?" Aunt Dee asked him while picking up the schoolwork he had pushed off his lap and spat on.

Winny dropped his head between his arms; Aunt Dee rubbed his back until his wheezing slowed.

"They dumped water on me," he mumbled, smelling deep-fried chicken and smoked ham on her smock and staring at her stitched name. "They said, 'Stupid.' 'Retard.'"

Uncle Ren's truck rattled into the space choked out by weeds summer storms surged after they had soaked through the mobile-home park's rust and mold. He laid his welding gloves on the hood, kissed Dee, and sat his thermos and a grocery bag on the ground. "Friday-night goodies." He pulled out daisies tied off by twine, a small blue pouch, and crayons and a coloring book. He handed the flowers to Dee.

"Ziegler's?" she asked.

"They said the sunflowers are so tall now the bees're nuts for 'em." He dumped into his thermos the pouch's blue powder and, after swirling it, offered it to Winny who gulped it down. His greasy finger ran under the flavor. "E-lec-tric B-lue." He kissed Winny's hair. "I don't know no flavor like that. Do you?"

Winny giggled and gulped again. His lips and teeth belonged to winter.

Uncle Ren slid the coloring book and crayons to Winny. He whispered to Dee, "She said it might help. Maybe he can do it by himself."

The three of them looked over the cover's cartoon and recommended reading level: FOR AGES 3 TO 5—younger than Winny.

Winny turned to a page.

"I've always liked elephants." Aunt Dee emphasized the puffy letters, one by one, under the outline. "They're so peaceful and strong. They're some of the smartest animals out there." She raised her arm and trumpeted at Winny.

Holding the bag's last item, Uncle Ren walked to the toolbox in the truck bed.

"I'll go get the food." Aunt Dee shuffled for the backyard and, returning the car port, held a jar. She shook the red liquid inside and said the sugar water was fresh.

Uncle Ren hammered under a corner and dangled wires for the hummingbird feeder that hovered outside the curtains of the living room where Winny slept and could not stop peering through.

· · ·

After his walk at the river, Winny stops in the foyer of the building with the rooftop bar. Birds fly over—none of them his cardinal. Across the street, Russ's desk lamp flicks off; his office darkens; he emerges, juggling briefcase and phone, from the rehab center. Winny slides deeper into the foyer as a delivery man nearly bumps his dolly into Winny, and the doors behind them close. Winny notices a sign taped to the glass—HIRING – APPLY INSIDE, rushes past the foyer, approaches the front desk, and asks about the sign.

"Um…" The hostess shrugs at a woman in a blouse and slacks pivoting for the front.

"What kind of job are you looking for?" the woman shouts, halfway to Winny.

"Anything." He pauses as the waiters organize menus, run through computer screens, arrange magnets for the night's specials, and talk rapidly back and forth. "But not out here."

The woman crosses her arms. "Can you prep food?"

Winny's head wavers no-yes.

"Wash dishes?"

"Yes, ma'am. My friend Makenzay and I help out with that where we live. Trash and clean-up, too."

The woman's eyes narrow. "It's minimum wage. Weekends and holidays, especially Sunday brunch. They split all tips."

"When can I start?"

"Do you have references?"

"Russ. My counselor," Winny stutters.

"Are you from across the street?"

After Winny nods yes, the woman's jaw juts. "No. He sent someone here a while back. No." Her heels clack as she strides under a chandelier and staircase and toward the kitchen and a kindle in an oven.

When Winny reaches the rehab center and signs in, his phone buzzes: YOU LIBRARY ONE HOUR. He stops in the Quiet Room where Makenzay cradles her laptop.

"Russ was looking for you."

"Did he say anything?"

She slides on her headphones and resumes her video game.

Winny bites his nails and flops himself and his backpack on the sofa. He opens his book and practices tonight's passage. A lightning bolt zaps the talons on Makenzay's griffin, which sparkle before the griffin strikes demons blocking a tower leading to planets, suns, and constellations. An owl with a gray beard and a monocle opens the tower's gates and congratulates the griffin, which roars and electrifies it wings. Winny spins toward the windows. Strands of lights snap on at the rooftop bar—small globes wiped clean and their cores shining through.

He taps Makenzay's shoulder. "You got any cash?"

"Dude, seriously?" She pauses the game and rips off her headphones. Leaving for her room, she yells, "Shouldn't you be doing homework?"

"Like you?"

She tosses her wallet at him and flips off a demon's chains grounding her griffin.

"Do you want to get a drink?"

Her head cocks.

"Not that."

"I am in the middle of something." Her eyes motion to her game.

"Take a study break. Like me."

• • •

The hostess who earlier greeted Winny says to him, "Yes?"

"We want drinks."

"The bar down here is for our guests with reservations. And we're all booked for tonight. I'm sorry."

"Not here. Upstairs. I've seen them out there."

"Our rooftop bar is open now…yes." She inspects Winny and Makenzay. "For happy hour."

Makenzay smirks while chewing gum.

"How do we get there?" Winny asks.

The hostess twirls her pen. "Elevator is over there. The stairs are behind that column."

The couple who rode up with Winny and Makenzay heads to a table in the middle of the rooftop chilled by the evening breeze. A waitress recognizes the woman in sequined jeans and unlatching a purse quilted in gold, and she twists the nearby heater's knob while confirming the couple's Tuesday-night usuals. Makenzay picks her scarf's frayed ends. Winny wanders the crowd, table games, and rainbow lights cascading from roof to ground and trees, rocks, and grass. Makenzay taps a stool at the bar; Winny tells her to take it before he searches for the waterfall. She squeezes into a napkin a gum wad as bright as her coat's patches and the prints of koi swimming across her leggings. Winny slides between her and a woman who leaves and switches her cocktail for her phone.

"Would you get us two cherry Cokes?"

"When I get some service." Makenzay wiggles her fingers at the bartender. "Where you going?"

Winny points to an L-shaped corner and scraps of sunlight on the top-most brick.

"Don't leave me here by myself."

"OK." He leans on the bar.

"How was the Hyatt?"

"I made it."

"That's a check in the good box."

"But I was late."

"Sorry."

"Then I found something else near us. It's here."

"Here? Yuck." Makenzay makes a face.

"It was also minimum wage but with tips they'd split. But nope."

After their drinks arrive, Makenzay digs for the cherry buried in the ice; Winny stirs the rust-colored syrup until it clouds the glass. They toast and consider sharing appetizers because it's pasta night at the center—the cans of spaghetti from food drives when Makenzay stayed at a women's shelter are, she reiterates, better—but Winny doesn't want to. Evening spreads at the bottom of the sky; lights flash behind the L-shaped corner over Makenzay's shoulder; and a bird streaks crimson toward a door.

Winny snatches napkins and nearly knocks the dispenser into the beer flights next to him. "You got a pen?"

Makenzay hands him one from her coat before he scribbles down the time and place and jogs to the corner.

A cook, grease covering his apron, stacks crates printed SAN JUAN CAPISTRANO FARMS arching over a California mission and snow-capped mountains, fields of artichokes, and swallows tying bows atop expiration dates. The cook exits through the door into the building; his shoes clomp down stairs. The outside light clicks off.

In darkness and under the smoke-gray mound of twigs and leaves—a circle of earth in the secluded corner—Winny stands with his candle of a phone. He steps closer, his neck raising, the cold night picking up around him, and he shields the phone's screen from the cardinals chirping inside their nest. When the fifteen-till-the-library alarm blinks and chimes, he smothers the sounds and words. Napkin and pen in his other hand, and before Makenzay tugs his arm as crowd noise spills their way, Winny steps closer, yet far away enough for the birds to ignore him, as though he sees and hears them through glass, from inside a room, for the first time.

· · ·

"Well, hello there." Russ's smile exaggerates his teeth's gap after he opens the study room's door, his pastel shirt as pink as

Makenzay's blush and Winny's cheeks. "Come on in. We saved you seats. Thanks for joining us this evening and gracing us with your presence. We're so happy you made it."

Makenzay snorts, sliding between new residents from the rehab center. "We had to get our assignments."

"From the other side of town? Or all the way in the Outer Banks?" Russ keeps grinning, settling into his chair.

"Did you know the front desk still has up Valentine's Day?" Makenzay asks. "It's almost Easter, and I said something to Pat while we were there. Not that I'm getting back into any of that holiday-committee stuff ever again. I just can't, Russ."

The big man agrees.

"Hey, y'all." Makenzay waves to everyone. "We're here now. And we're ready to show you what we got." Her fist pumps the air.

"That's what I want to hear." Russ clicks his pen.

"But I'll go last."

Everyone laughs.

Winny looks at Russ who, at the head of the table, glances over his glasses.

"OK, who's next? Rasheeda?"

"Me? Oh, I don't know."

"Yes, ma'am. Come on now. Let's do this."

The young woman sitting next to Makenzay tugs her braids and mumbles. She stops speaking, and the pages stick to her when she hides her face. "I can't. It's so hard."

"Be with that for a second. Start again when you're ready."

Rasheeda blows into her hands before shaking them out. She stumbles over the word *Corinthians* but then smooths it, the chapter and verse numbers, and the first sentence, after which she smiles, her voice like a runner content with her pace, while reading about clay jars that, when broken, cannot be repaired yet reveal what's hidden.

"Very good," Russ says after she finishes, clapping with everyone.

"That's something he gave me when I got here," Winny says to Rasheeda. "It took me a while. Congratulations."

Rasheeda mouths *Thank you* and folds her paper.

At Winny's first study session, the center's van dropped him off; he hadn't earned walking. Russ met him outside the library's mosaic glowing turquoise and gold among autumn leaves. Winny followed Russ to the middle of Circulation and the last free table and chairs amid students, parents, and kids staying until closing time. Winny recognized faces he had seen on the streets. The big man pulled a folder and pencils from his briefcase and took Winny to the Children's section.

"My kids love this book. They check it out every time we're here." He revealed a cover: a teddy bear driving a plane in the morning, a boat at noon, a car at dusk, and a spaceship among stars. He pulled more books off the shelves. All his selections for Winny were large print and illustrated.

They cruised the shelves—the lanky white guy in a hoodie, baggy jeans, tattoos, and bloodshot; and Russ, stout and black with a beard and dressed in slacks, shirt, and tie. Winny wandered into Periodicals where he flipped through an art magazine; he kept his thumb on the article demonstrating the process of inking Japanese scrolls.

"Do you want that?" Russ asked.

"I wasn't gonna steal it."

"Would you like to use it for practice?"

Winny nodded yes.

"Bring it. Let's get to work." Russ returned to the table where they had set up.

A few patrons stared at Winny leaving the racks and carrying under his arm the magazine opened to strokes becoming, line by line, a river, a raven, and a poem.

After Rasheeda's turn, the new residents flanking Makenzay read their assignments and receive feedback and next week's practice.

Russ says, "Let's take a break." He calls Winny aside. "Mark Ruiz from the Hyatt called me."

"The bus never came. I walked the whole way."

"He said you said that. What did you and Makenzay do before this?"

"We got some Cokes from across the street."

"That's it?"

"We had cherry in them."

"All right. We'll talk more tomorrow."

One by one, the class returns.

"Everybody feeling better after getting a stretch or something to drink? Maybe a snack to hold you over?" Russ checks something off his paper.

Makenzay swirls a vending-machine coffee and raises her eyebrows at Winny who shrugs.

"Who would like to go next?"

Winny raises his hand. "I will." His legs pumping, he slides his bird book onto the table, rotates his shoulders, coughs. His finger traces his passage; he mutters. "Hold on." His fingers stop tracing and twitch. He shows something to Makenzay, and before she answers, he says, "Never mind. I got it. Thanks though." He shifts in his seat and clears his throat; his tattooed hands flatten on the table. "'Cardinals are red. They are the state bird. They have orange beaks. The male has black stripes on his wings. The female is bigger than him, but he is prettier than the female.'"

The group chuckles.

"'They have four chicks. They are gray and fuzzy. They make sounds. They all live in a nest. It is like small trees tied together.' That was my one simile."

"Yes, it was." Russ smiles. "Good."

Returning to his passage, Winny swallows. "'They live close to me. They live across the street. They live on a roof.'" He stops on the spot. "This is my one complex sentence."

"Let's hear it."

"'I see them every day at the same time, but it took me a long time to find them.'"

Home Improvement

Starting with floors and paint, he renovates the kitchen after a
month of smaller projects while he's on leave. But do we need
track lighting? his wife asks. Their yellow lab stands half sentinel,
half coworker who never works because of drink, food, nap, or
bathroom breaks; Heidi whines whenever Everett whines,
crushes his thumb, glues his cheek to backsplash tile, slices a
chunk between his palm and other thumb, nearly blows up
cabinets and counters when he re-lines the gas; and bobs her
head as though she agrees with his diatribes about CEOs,
celebrities, and tenured professors making ends meet. In the
winter sun, the room whitens—morning sky bare, snow
everywhere. Liz says everything looks great, take a break. The
house hushes but remains curled on Everett's chest and in his gut
alongside his weight gain since they cut the gym. Furloughs
remain in effect… He stops reading the email and spies a wire
poking from grout and split like the Devil's tongue. Liz kisses
him, leaves for work. He waits until her car turns the block before
rummaging in his toolbox. The house tells him to open the wall
where the wire disappears into a dark he must climb through
after he chisels out a square like a vault.

Among insulation and load-bearing beams, the house follows
him, shows him where he's not done enough—incomplete

patches, rough spots, faulty connections—tells him he must carry more; Liz will abandon him, if he does not. She's been on the computer more, alone in the bedroom more, Everett says to himself. She may have a different bank account, the house adds, offering up rotting corners for him to inspect. Half is yours, but all will be hers. He crosses a gap into which gloves from his overalls' pockets collapse. Spring is next week, the house continues, but ice will stay in place, will not thaw with your salt alone. Nails snag Everett's shirt. He searches his hips: his hammer left near the breadbox where Liz will find it when she comes home for lunch. The house spreads shadows, spins Everett toward wet pipes and away from Liz before she speaks to her brother on the phone—He's done so much for us already—and spins him toward her, loose back-porch screen door as bait, when, after Liz asks Heidi where Everett went and watches her claw the varnished floor, she says their months have broken down since he's been home. He can't manage it all.

Sounds about right, Everett reckons as cold pools around him. Patrick has a beef with me. That one Easter he dressed like a bunny for his kids, and before the picture was taken, I placed chocolate eggs under his tail, making it look like he took a shit. Shivering, Everett peers at the master bedroom's corner where he measured for ceiling mirrors, a glitter ball, and a stripper's pole— if Liz wants to dust off her old days of paying off student loans —but stopped because of resale value and the creepy neighbor next door. Am I in the basement? he asks, finding no furnace or pilot light. Need a better weather sealant, he notes, nearly knocking his head off in a tunnel growing longer and slimmer. He's a snug fit; hears Liz tell him, when depression circles him, running and meditation are free; and slides down until his feet can go no further. Resting on his back, he glances up at grass and tree roots. Flowers glow like stars. October's seeds, he says, pleased with last fall's efforts but can't reach them because a lid slides over him. The house twists tighter, tells him if he stays put, he can't fail anywhere else.

Four bells appear above him. The right one rings. Patrick's voice says Everett will go blind either from using his laser level on all his projects or from masturbating, which is the real reason he's upgrading the bathroom—sound-proof padding, faster wireless. Set it aside for a while. You two come over and just chill while I set up shelves for my comics and action figures. The bell jostles again: I'll need your laser level. Heidi barks from a middle bell. I'm down here, you good girl, Everett cries. The bark-bell intensifies. One bark for yes, two for no, OK? One bark from the bell. Everett wipes his eyes. Are you alone? Two barks. Is Liz there? One bark. Everett sniffles, swallows. Can you get her? A rapid succession of ringing soon stops. Heidi? Heidi? A sleep-inducing tone overtakes the left bell. Everett's boss praises his skills and company loyalty and really, deeply wishes HR policies held employees' best interests, but her hands are tied until the economy improves. Everett's fat palm snaps it off. From the other middle bell, Liz's voice emerges. Heidi's going crazy— there's a snake.

New appliance boxes shield Liz and Heidi. Shovel in hand, Everett peers between garden rocks and buds under frost. Scales stiffen; a reddish mass slithers. Maybe we can cover it with a dish, Everett says. You're not using my Tupperware for that. What about an old one?—it's time to replace those. Your sisters chipped in for those from our registry, and they're old but fine. My sisters or the dishes? Everett smirks. Hissing intensifies in the sun's warm single stretch. Liz says they've pissed it off more, and she doesn't care if it's not poisonous. We could give it to the kid across the street, Everett says—he won that science fair for climate change, I think, and… Liz strikes the shovel hard; the body flops around. Heidi jumps in for the head but jumps out like jumping in was a bad idea. Liz thinks it's too early for the season. Maybe it found the crawlspace, Everett suggests. Do you think there's a nest of them? she asks, holding his wrist. He heads for the house. I'll find out.

Names of Horses

"Now I won't," she stutters through tears, shrugging off her backpack and slamming her door shut. She flings the book from the shelf to her bed and finds the pages her parents helped her clothes-pin—adults and children spreading their fingers across horses, their thumbs and pinkies measuring, from noses to ears, hooves to shoulders, over manes, above *Hands high and Hands wide*, the caption's bite lasting after she read it then and returns to it now. She kicks the book off her bed and tells the toy horses lining her walls she won't be able to now. "I will never…" Her voice breaks. "I can't now."

Her mom knocks and sets the backpack on the desk. "Persi, are you OK?"

"I'm not going." She buries her head in pillows; tightens into a small, thin S floating between the bedcover's green hills and ponies and horseshoes and stars sparkling on the ceiling.

"Why?"

"Because."

Her mother sifts through the backpack, pulling the spindle attached to the zipper, and checks the lunch bag, homework, and a stack of cards and drawings. "But this is so nice of your class and Mrs. Cremmins." She covers her mouth when she reaches the last drawing. "Oh God, no. Oh, I am sorry. How did Mrs. Cremmins not catch this?"

The door from kitchen to garage opens and closes.

Her mother throws the drawing on the desk and, in the hallway, halfway to the bedroom, meets a shadow who embraces her as she leans on its shoulder.

Persi cringes at the drawing splayed open to its stick figure saying she could not touch a horse unless she asked for doll hands for her birthday.

Her father nudges the drawing toward him, his face falling briefly sad, before smiling at her. He loosens his tie and sits next to her. "You should go. The horses want to see you. They've been waiting all day for you. I just know it." He smooths her hair as he peeks at the book cracked on its spine.

"How do you know?" she asks, sliding her wrists under her shirt.

"You'll have to find out when you're there."

* * *

The road jars her in the back of the car—the stables closer, no longer a dusky square floating on the horizon and filled with horses she named without knowing their names, seeing their colors and markings on the website she told her parents about, asking to go, hoping. She told her classmates she was going for her birthday before leaving for a long vacation when the other website had enough donations for her surgery. The boy she liked said he would get robot hands, maybe like hers, and they could hold hands while swinging or sharing snacks, and his superhero hands could take down the moon, draw it complete for her— front and the sides no one on Earth sees—and set it back before anyone missed it.

"Pull over, Dad, please." Persi opens the door, before her father stops by the roadside, and rushes for grass and wildflowers raised by spring. Her feet squishing the ground, and among mud and yellow bulbs surrounding her shins, she hunches, covers her stomach, and dry-heaves. She looks up and into a long-limbed forest where, as in her dreams in bed or at her desk, a horse could emerge from fog hiding its legs beneath its knees and stagger toward her palms sometimes there and sometimes, at the end of her wrists, only air.

"Sweetie?" Her mother stands behind her; rubs her back; hands her water.

"I'm sick."

"We can go back."

Persi breathes in coming rain, soft leaves, and soil and leans up when whinnies echo ahead.

Her father's fingers drum the car roof. "We're close, but we can go back if you want."

Neighs answer neighs, and Persi, dodging and leapfrogging snails, her shoes sliding into fresh shoots and roots, returns to the car, tightens her seatbelt, and nods OK.

After they pass through the main gate, they idle where a rider and a horse wait to cross the trail near a sign and its arrows pointing from silhouettes of a hiker, a bike, and car to a horse. The rider's hat bobs a thank you. Persi follows the rider's boots and jeans pulsing on the haunches colored like chocolate milk spilled across a pale sheet.

Her father lowers her window.

"I got it," she says, wedging her wrist on the button and sticking her head out until the rider and horse disappear under trees and then into a corral and its rails dividing them into segments, like her book cut up, until they stop in front of an open pen and become whole again. Persi rolls up her window when the rider curls off the horse's back and pats its snout and neck.

When the car stops alongside the shelter with the longest roof and, hitched on the opposite end, a pair of horses brushed by hand, she sinks deeper into her seat and hides from the window. She drifts behind her parents as they walk toward the woman holding a clipboard.

"Tell her your name." Her mom nudges her forward.

Head down, Persi shies away.

"It's your birthday, right?" the woman asks underneath her cap's FOUR LEGS ARE BETTER THAN TWO.

Persi slightly smiles as her mother squeezes her shoulders. "Yes."

"How old are you?"

"Eight."

Kids laugh as their horses trot.

"But at six-thirty-seven tonight."

Her parents and the woman chuckle.

Persi glimpses the pair of horses under the shelter. A man smooths their tails and runs his fingers over and through them like her classmates with their hair and fingers.

The woman offers the clipboard and pen to Persi's father. "We're happy y'all are here."

"Maybe we should get going," he says, nodding to dark-gray clouds and thunder in the distance.

The man under the shelter brings over the smaller horse to where Persi stands before he retrieves a step he sets on the ground and near the stirrups. After he digs in his pocket and opens his palm, the horse, dipped in rust save for white chipped off its ankles, munches away.

"Is that mine?"

"It sure is." The woman smiles at Persi and her parents.

"It's Persimmon Yuan-Winster." The nub of her left wrist motions at the clipboard. "But I go by Persi."

"Very nice to meet you. Are you ready?"

"Yes." She lets her parents help her to the step, but when she stands atop, her arms flutter off their help. She turns and briefly smiles at the camera her father holds in one hand while holding her mother's in the other. Persi waves a long-awaited wish.

But closer thunder scares horses in the corrals. Persi's horse shudders away from the step. The man who brought the horse bridles it back to the stables alongside horses taken in as rain falls; he mutters, "Sorry" to Persi. Standing over the gap where her horse stood, Persi leans away where her arms were about to land and keeps from falling into more rain plinking on the shelter smothered by quick darkness and the murmurs of horses and handlers rushing in and around.

"Right, I understand, but we paid for this for today." Her father's voice rises in the downpour.

"I'm sorry. She can come back in September. We're booked through summer."

"Maybe she'll be done with therapy by then," her mother says.

"She might be able to grip the reins."

"We can make it work for her," the woman says.

"Persi, we'll have to come back after we see Dr. Hix, OK?"

But when her father asks, she's a small red dot heading for the stables and slanting in rain and wind. She peers into each pen, bending up or down, moving row to row, her shoes kicking up dust like the horses greeting her, turning away when she's near, or ignoring her except for their ears twisting in humidity and among her scuffling about. She bypasses Southpaw, Patches, and Mr. Dupree's Ecstasy, agreeing that their names match them but disagreeing when she cruises past Butternut Magic and Eugene, two plain boys side by side—not because their names are wrong but because she wishes she had been there to name them perfectly.

She stops at rust-colored legs chipped white at their ends and stares into the corner where the neck stretches for a tree. She runs outside, rain bursting, and circles the stable, her parents yelling as she splashes puddles, "Where are you going? We're leaving!" She leaps at the apples dangling from the branch, the horse throttling its head left to right, up and down, but she can't snap off stems. The horse whinnies and kicks clods; whinnies answer down the row. Thunder diminishes, but rain and gray stay. Persi crouches and gathers fallen apples in her shirt, dragging them in.

"Sweetie…"

"Persi?"

Between wrists and forearms, she balances an apple, extends it, and waits.

• • •

They pull into the garage, through a thin waterfall tumbling off the gutter, and a blanket around her, she sniffles into the kitchen, kicking off her muddy, wet shoes on the mat, her clothes sopped, her mother trailing behind and pleading with her that Persi can't risk another infection.

"Why'd you do that?" she asks again, but softer than in the car, carrying hot tea and fresh clothes into the bedroom.

"I didn't know his name."

"And?" Her father helps take off her socks.

"He ate so quick." She dresses herself in pajamas, shaking her head at her parents who step back. "I didn't see it."

Her mother readies the trashcan to catch the cards and drawings before she slides them in.

"No. I want to look at them."

Her mother stops and glances over; her father shrugs.

"Brandon made one for me." Persi's eyes narrow on the top of the stack.

Her mother fans them and pulls one warped from blue watercolor. "This one?"

"Yes."

Her mother blushes. "It looks like his."

"It does." Her father wiggles Persi's toes. "Need anything else?"

"No."

After they close the door, she faces the card's sky backdropping Earth and stars outlined in pencil and drenched in yellow marker.

HAPPY BIRTHDAY PERSI!!! I hope you see horses. I hope you touch one. I hope to touch one too. But I have allergies. See you at school on Monday.

His scribbles found space leftover from his drawing of two horses, like cave paintings, dominating the inside and the strip of land he placed them on.

P.S. Promise to tell me what it's like.

"Dinner, Persi!"

Her father lights the last candle as she turns the corner and thinks about what she'll tell Brandon. His whiskers tickled my arms. Like I thought they would. Her parents pull out her chair and lay out the silverware they help her with. He slobbered all over me. My wrists and arms were sticky. He was muddy. He only cared about the apple. I don't even know his name. Her parents sing over pizza and cake. But I didn't have to ask him to come to me.

Strike Sides

The two of them bounding off and chatting like crows, they find shadows behind the carport, after the wake settles in with food and drink, and the taller cousin, gum smacking, flashes his fingers, and the short, thickset cousin pops toward the numbers hovering before him. The short cousin's lips part; his tongue clicks, foaming from beer and cheese; his eyebrows, rolling up from his glasses, pulse *Lotta money.* And then Mitch dabs his forehead and wipes humidity off his glasses and glances at his husband in the living room; at the woods behind the house; at the scars along Danell hyping the amount.

"Right?" Danell whispers, pulling Mitch back to him. "I know a guy who can get us that much. Probably more." He tongues his gum into his other cheek after he peers around the carport as other cousins roll Grandma Doesheena into the living room, carpet briefly catching under her wheelchair, the crowd circling her way. "We split it fifty-one, forty-nine."

Mitch flinches. "Hell no."

"It's only one percent, and he's my contact."

"One percent with that amount is no drop in the bucket." Mitch's voice fades when Mike turns from the living room window and searches for him. "They're technically mine. My name was listed first when it was read off."

"We're going by that?" Danell spits his gum into honeysuckle. "Grandpa Ike promised to place the Derby one on top, which we saw today. And there was no matches left in it because he used them up. Thus proving…"

"He knew you'd burn down everything." Mitch's head cranks toward the living room, the old organ churning out a hymnal, and off-key voices thrumming. "You have no witnesses to prove any of this."

"I can tell you it was after church one Easter Sunday. Aunt Kath wasn't knocked up with you yet."

"Autheil comes before Richert. The lawyer read it that way. And I know a thing or two about legal documents by now." Mitch stuffs his hands in his pockets. "Fifty-one, forty-nine…me."

"Fine." Chuckling, Danell dabs the summer heat. "I want you and Mike to get yours. Whatcha gonna do with yours?"

"State and court fees and attorneys add up." Mitch checks the living room when clapping increases and the circle hugs Grandma Doesheena. "And we want to plant something under him. College fund or medical expenses. Hell…clothes so kids at school won't make fun of him. Nothing fancy or sticking out. Just want him to fit in."

"I get that."

"You?"

"Help out with Carol's mortgage." He opens a shed and rummages on a shelf. "She's underwater."

"Damn." Mitch's head nearly twists off. "I could never do that for my ex's mother." He pats Danell's arm. "But that's good. She was good to you."

Another hymn starts, and Mike drifts over to the kitchen sink; smiles at Mitch and Danell; and drinks, fills his cup, drinks, fills. Mitch heads for a car parked out front and then, with a folder under his arm, inside the house through the front door, bypasses the living room for the kitchen, and meets Mike. Danell grabs a roll of trash bags off the shelf; sneaks through the back screen door; collects discarded paper plates, cups, and utensils; and joins the circle in the living room as the song stops, the singing echoes, Mitch and Mike share the name and photo of the boy they want to adopt, and Danell wraps his arms around Grandma Doesheena and then his girlfriend and her kids. His eyes cross Mitch's before rising to their grandfather's office upstairs.

• • •

Danell seals the tub under the kitchen light, slides it alongside the stack, and types in the spreadsheet, saving its inventory and notes—origin and history; quality; date ranges; and features of its matchbooks and -boxes, such as the Frank Lloyd Wright series and the flip-top B-52s soaring between sunset and Pearl Harbor —and updating estimates he tracked over the years. He takes the lid off the next tub, flatter and wider than the others, and smiles at the matchbooks displayed like butterflies under glass.

Trina's chair creaks when the dugouts on TV clear for a brawl; her baby boy kicks and snorts. "Bedtime, girls."

The two girls, camped in front of the baseball game, moan but put away their toys, books, and blankets; skip into the kitchen; and cozying up to Danell, ooh and ah and ask questions. They ho-hum at the household products and flour, tobacco, and sugar companies but jump up and down at moose, pandas munching bamboo, and the American Spaniel Club parti-colored cocker perched as on a hunt. Danell gently untacks it from the display board and, with tweezers, rolls it over: three maroon-tipped matches. He types *Intact x 3* into the spreadsheet, followed by *Strike Sides Condition Excellent*.

"Good night, Danell," the girls chime, hugging him.

"Good night," he says, kissing them before they run off with Trina to the bathroom. He blows kisses toward Trina who mouths *I love you* and, with her boy's chubby hand, waves goodnight.

He sets the smallest tub on the table and sneezes at the puffs of dust, but plugging his nose, stops it from dripping over the contents—a container, no bigger than a brick, inside the tub cushioned by foam and packing tissue. He washes his hands, double-checks they're dry, and like holding an egg, lifts the container from the tub. "Bingo," he mutters, placing the matchbox at eye level. He inspects the all-around sides—no graphics or words missing; none of the horses faded; none of the laurels' flowers or leaves rubbed off; no gold on the champions list flaked; the Triple Crown winners still bold; the track and grandstand printed on the lid in pristine condition. He checks underneath for the red serial number. He finds a similar matchbox on a website and reviews its estimate and the estimate he entered for KENTUCKY DERBY 125TH ANNIVERSARY – LIMITED EDITION – MINT. His drumroll on the table crescendoes into slapping and scooting it across the linoleum.

"You OK?" Trina mumbles behind a toothbrush, peeking around the kitchen corner.

"More than." He grabs his phone, sends the matchbox's photo, and texts <Lots of zeroes for this.> He grins when Mitch replies with dollar bills and a smiley face wearing sunglasses.

· · ·

Mike peeks over Aesop's Fables. "So I'm guessing good news, huh?"

Mitch kisses him again. "He found the golden ticket." His phone buzzes seconds later. "And he found the National Parks series, college football bowls, including the Cotton where Grandma Doe met Grandpa Ike, and the pillbox series of coastal getaways." He zooms in—a wrap-around scene of a Victorian house bordered by a green lawn, a party, and sprays from the Atlantic Ocean; the other with a roller coaster jutting up between palm trees, a pier, and the Hollywood sign, orange groves, and snow-capped mountains. "Danell says they're in pristine condition except for the Shenandoah Park one. The headwaters of the James have been rubbed off. But what we got is solid."

Mike tugs the bedsheet. "And you don't want any of them?"

"It was fun seeing them when I was young. He loved showing them to me. But I'm not young anymore. And he's not around to show them to me."

"OK." Mike flips to the next story.

Mitch clicks off his lamp, mumbles "Night," and fidgets. He turns on his back and stares at the four blue-white squares as a full moon stretches from the window across the ceiling, turning the muntins into bright X's burning paths through shadows. "You think I should keep them."

"I have nothing from my family. Kim and Mark fought over it all and made it all about them. And they weren't even selling any of it. They only wanted it so no one else could have it. But yes, I wanted something. My father's pocket watch. My mother's piano books. I would've taken my father's pen he used to write to me from the nursing home. He sucked on it near the end. Anything. And none of it for money."

"It's not about money."

Mike snorts. "Babe…"

"It's about our kid's future. The sale helps that."

"He wanted you to have them. And Danell. Both of you." Mike sets the bookmark on the page after the frog agrees to carry the scorpion across the stream. "Your mom mentioned to me at the funeral you loved going up to Ike's office and having him show his collection to you. She said every time you visited you couldn't wait to do it. And Danell was always next to you." He turns off his lamp and turns on his phone's alarm. "She said Danell asked to take one to his AA graduation. Not a valuable one but one that meant he kept his promise of being focused. Your grandpa said no."

"He didn't trust him. But that didn't bother Danell." Mitch rubs his beard. "I mean, he was hurt a little bit, but he understood why."

"But Ike said yes to him in his will." Yawning, Mike pivots a small fan closer to him. "She said when you came out and told him you wanted nothing to do with them."

"Like I said, I grew up. I grew into my skin."

"OK." He kisses Mitch's shoulder. "See you in the mornin'. Sweet dreams."

Mitch stares at the ceiling. The blue-white squares fade to purple-blue, deepening in the room, and the voice of Grandpa Ike follows behind. "What did you want to tell me?" he asked that day, sleet cracking the air, ice slicing the windows. And shaking, Mitch told him, finding bravery Danell never had to find, and Ike, smiling, his eyepatch blacker in the cold air, replied, "I don't understand…why not girls. I don't support it, but I also won't get in your way." Mitch closed the office door and stopped in the hall where a light, brightened by winter and nothing on the trees stopping it, landed like rocks underwater where an animal could cross when it was ready.

. . .

A young man in a baggy black shirt opens the screen door. "Yeah?"

"Is Carol home?"

"Who you?"

Danell peeks over the young man's shoulder. A woman around the same age lounges in a t-shirt on the couch's pull-out bed and swipes her phone. "I'm her ex-son-in-law."

"Which one?"

"The good-looking one. Is she at Matty's?"

"She don't work there no more."

"Will she be home today?"

The young man lights a cigarette and blows it in Danell's face. "Don't know."

"Tomorrow?"

The young man shrugs.

"What do you know?"

The young man's lip curl can't discern Danell's response as a question or an insult.

"Tell her Danell came by. And it's a good thing. A very good thing. Can you do that for me?" He glimpses the young woman taking selfies while music changes. "Please."

The young man throws his chin at the envelope Danell holds. "That for her?"

"What's your name?" Danell stares at the young man as he takes a long, slow drag and flashes a tattoo on his left shoulder. "Did you get that in case you forgot?" He smirks at the script CHARLZ N CHARGE arcing over a pot leaf, the silhouette of a stripper on her pole, and two lightsabers crossing blades.

Charlz's scrawny body puffs up as much as it can. Holding a cigarette, he stabs the air when he spits *Pfffft* before the screen door squeaks shut and music cranks up.

Danell starts his car and, checking his rearview mirror—no changes in Carol's house or her driveway or street—idles in the alley nestled among gravel, concrete, and rust; the treatment plant; and the remains of a factory where, among a disintegrating wall's jagged shadows and the odors of water purified and circled back, Carol slapped Danell, warning him to get help or lose everything, starting with her daughter. Baseball bat in hands, she chased him there—broken red brick like fallen fire; busted mortar like ashes—after he showed up at her place looking for Alyssa. Carol gave him the name of her sponsor. "You call him now, or I call the cops on you. I'll even let you call him from my phone. But you do it now or else." She led him to the phone in her kitchen; her bedroom's door shut when Danell entered, Alyssa having watched from behind it.

He turns on the windshield wipers when headlights cut through drizzle and stop at the curb by Carol's house. Charlz runs out, checks up and down the street, passes something through the passenger window in exchange for something he slides into his shorts, and struts back in as the car's brake lights blur driving away. Danell checks his phone's time, reclines his seat more, and falls asleep under rain.

After his phone wakes him, he checks the screen and answers. "Hi there."

"I thought you was sitting there."

"You home?"

"I am."

Danell leans up and rolls down his window to clouds moving off the sky and Carol, phone in hand, waving from her front porch. "I have something for you. I just want to give it to you then I'll be on my way."

"Everything all right?"

"Yeah, it is."

His boots squish mud and puddles in the yard on his way to the porch where he offers the envelope to Carol. As she wipes her eyes and whispers thank you in his ear, he hugs her. No catches, he tells her—she gave him more than he can return. The rest is numbers.

. . .

During his lunch break, Mitch reads an update from the lawyer and the adoption agency—Still in a holding pattern until after some more hoops are jumped that are out of our control. Hang tight. After Labor Day we'll get there.—and confirms the money has transferred into the account from DANELL J. RICHERT. He scans the auction summary Danell forwarded, swallows hard when he sees the collection's prices, and smiles down each row, description, opening and closing bid, and net after fees and taxes until he reaches the bottom. Above the set of India railroad companies; Glasgow pubs and hotels, when Grandpa Ike and Grandma Doe visited after he returned from the Korean War with both legs but one eye; and the incomplete set of 1963 TWA Global Destinations, which garnished the most bids but lowest amount, the matchbox with two rabbits in a circle, like curls of black and white inks, sold at a price that can neither alleviate monthly expenses nor contribute to college savings. But when Mitch sees the sale of the rabbits, his lunch flavors fade; his stomach cramps; his throat dries more. He dumps his salad in the waste basket, tosses the container into his cubicle's corner, and picks at his coffee cup.

A coworker knocks. "Here's HeathFirst." She leans until he sees her. "Mitch?"

"Yeah. Thanks. I'll get to it."

"You OK?"

"We're still meeting at four today, right?" He sits up and logs into his work email.

"We are."

"I'll see you then."

Her chin lowers toward the packet she placed in his basket. "It needs a once-over before then."

He drags out a roll of memo flags and uncaps a highlighter. "With bells on." He lays out a fake smile, waits until she leaves, and returns to his email and the rabbits matchbox. <You threw this in?> he texts Danell. He raises his phone to his computer screen magnifying the matchbook and sends the photo. <I didn't know about that, and had I known, no way. Not that one.> He picks his thumb as he stares at his phone.

Danell stole the rabbits matchbox when Grandpa Ike and Grandma Doe vacationed to their annual river trip. He showed Mitch the key taped behind the velvet board displaying Ike's military medals. He unlocked the cabinet, and the matchbooks and -boxes inside glowed in summer light like a miniature city advertising fantasies, illusions, celebrities, sports, and trivia on its roofs and sides. Danell picked up the rabbits, as big as a deck of cards, and held its yin-yang swirl, saying Grandpa Ike wouldn't notice it missing because he had better ones. Mitch stared the rabbits and then the rest of the collection, hesitated, but nodded after Danell swiped it. And unfurling his fist, Danell paired firecrackers alongside the rabbits.

Mitch closes his personal email and the browser. He highlights and flags a passage in the packet about suicide and opiate addiction rising during the recession and their impacts on insurance. He suggests in the margins amplifying the human factor in the local communities more than strategies for recouping portfolio losses. He snatches his phone when it buzzes.

<Broccoli with cheese or roots medley tonight?> Mike texts.

<Whatever pairs well with vodka.>

<Long day?>

Mitch's computer blips HEALTHFIRST MEETING: FIFTEEN MINUTES. <I gotta go.> He gathers the packet and a pen and removes his laptop from its desk monitor. As he waits for a print-out, he dials Danell who cuts off his voicemail.

"What's up?"

"You sold the rabbits matchbox."

"Uh…did I? I don't remember it in there."

"You did."

"How much did we get for it?"

"I wish I'd known you included it. It was my favorite."

"Do you want more for it? I'll give you my cut of it if you do. I can pull over and pull it up on my phone. And I can swing by your place this weekend."

Coworkers file into the conference room.

"I'll talk to you later."

The first slide glows on the screen—a graph depicting quality of life steadily declining and financial burdens increasing; the number of red hearts and dollar bills representing a happiness scale reduced from seven to one-half hearts and dollar bills reduced to coins. The lights dim as the presentation begins. Mitch is not the last to arrive, but he sits at the back, feeling all eyes inside and outside the room landing on him, as though he is.

• • •

The backdoor clangs open, and Danell lowers his ball cap and slinks in his seat when Charlz barges out and pulls the grease trap to the dumpster. After Charlz dumps the trap, leans against the wall, texting and smoking, and heads into the restaurant, Danell calls Carol. "You're right. He's at work."

"I've changed my mind. You don't have to do anything about it."

"That money ain't his."

"If I call the cops, he'll go back in."

"That's where he needs to be."

"My granddaughter will never forgive me. It took me years to get her back in my life. He's probably spent it by now. Maybe a better car. He asked me to help with that the other day."

"Doesn't matter. He stole it from you. It's yours."

"It's too late, Danell. I'll call his counselor. Just let it go."

He glares at the restaurant's back door and its light, half exposed to the coming night inside its rusted cage, pulsing faint to full. His boots thump the concrete when he drops from his car. He slowly opens the door and surveys the room—bags of apples, onions, and potatoes; red and yellow bottles on shelves; counters; an opened walk-in freezer and mist floating out. Servers in the distance, behind a taller counter, move back and forth through grill smoke and clanging silverware and dishes. He steps one foot in, holding the back door ajar, and pauses for the flow of sounds and comings and goings. Between a waitress and another busboy at a table wedged in the middle of the restaurant, Charlz wipes down a booth. Danell moves deeper into the storeroom when no one in the kitchen turns his way and when Charlz turns his back to Danell and dips his rag in a bucket.

"This isn't the front."

Danell glances at a man appearing from the walk-in freezer and rolling a cart of hamburger patties. "I didn't think it was."

The man cocks his head. "How'd you not see it? Big neon sign out front." He trails Danell to the back door, nods a *See ya, weirdo*, and slams the door shut.

As he cruises to the front, Daniel passes the window where Charlz cleans a table. They see each other; Charlz sneers; Danell snarls. The manager approaches Charlz and motions to tables they slide together; he arranges six chairs around the tables and holds up a number to Charlz who, before finding two chairs, leers at the window where Danell stood.

"Where's the envelope?" Danell yells, bypassing the hostess's welcome and driving straight for Charlz.

"Making more money than you right now."

"You give her back that goddamned money."

Customers twist in their seats. Waiters and waitresses stop. The hostess grabs her phone.

"What's going on?" the manager asks.

"You have a thief working for you. He stole money from my mother-in-law. It's hers, not his."

"She used to be your mother-in-law until you hit bottom." A smirk cuts Charlz's face. "I'll take care of her and her family because you can't."

Danell grips Charlz's shirt, stretching his name tag and the chili pepper stitched into it. Charlz reaches behind him into the dirty-dish tray and digs out a steak knife. The manager and nearby men wrangle Charlz and his stabbings off Danell who slumps to one knee and rasps, his hand covering bloodstains.

· · ·

A nurse motions to Mitch and Mike, and they come in, hug and kiss Trina, and say hi to her kids. The doctor rolls his stool back, snaps off his gloves and taps Danell, telling him they'll bring him some more pain meds. He consults Trina who smiles at Danell when he lifts a swollen thumbs-up.

"I gotta go to the admin desk about some paperwork," Trina says.

Mitch replies, "We'll watch him."

"Leave the kids," Mike adds.

Thank you she mouths, shoos the kids, save for her baby boy, toward Mitch and Mike, and shuffles out the room.

"Yay! Uncle Mike!"

Danell cringes as the girls scream and dance.

"Well…hotshot."

"Don't start." Danell's head flops away from Mitch and blushes as pink as the stitches crisscrossing his cheeks and nose. "At least wait until they come back with the stuff that'll numb me up real good."

"You made it to the Internet." Mitch holds up his phone. "'Both Richert and Urbay acknowledge the dispute was over money, but Richert qualified it was over a collection of matchbooks and matchboxes he inherited and sold after his grandfather died.'" He stops reading and, humming, scrolls down to the end. "'Dining service resumed after police and paramedics showed up. No restaurant guests were injured.' Everybody got their Friday night meals with some free entertainment." Mitch chuckles. "Remember when we went to that dinner theater with that Round Table cast, and they picked you to come on stage and do the sword battle?"

Danell's blackened eye flops a yes as he sucks ice chips.

"What was it you said to the Black Knight?"

"He yelled something from *Lord of the Rings*."

"I think it was Led Zeppelin."

"Ha ha. You two're funny." Danell winces, pulling the sheet over him. "Hey, girls? You wanna watch TV?"

They shake their heads yes and sit on the floor next to Mike. Danell flips the TV on and, grimacing, squiggles in bed. The next cartoon on the TV starts, and backgrounded by a circus, a rabbit handles a carrot like a cigar while promising a mustached prospector high on a diving board he'd never move the water tub beneath him while he plummets to the earth. The prospector doubts the rabbit but soon gives in and finishes his climb to the top where he reveals his swimming trunks and swim cap under his clothes.

"What was that thing the other day from you?"

Mitch pivots to Danell.

"One of the matchbooks?"

The prospector amplifies his bounces on the board, rising as high as the sun. The rabbit winks and tells the audience he had his fingers crossed when he promised.

"It was the one I wanted to keep."

"It got sold?"

"It did."

The rabbit's fat fluffy toe nudges away the water tub as the prospector accelerates toward Earth.

"I don't know if you told me or…"

"We never talked about it."

The rabbit feels guilty and, before the prospector crashes, returns with a small bottle which the prospector squeezes into.

"We just went forward with selling all of it. It was lumped in with all the others."

"Did Grandpa Ike promise it to you?"

"No."

"Uncle Mike, we're thirsty and hungry."

"OK."

Mike races the girls to the door.

"Which one was it again?" Danell asks, his voice scratchy.

"It doesn't matter." Mitch flips the channel from the cartoon to a sitcom. "We covered some fees and some of our lawyer with the sale."

"Man, that's so good. I'm glad to hear that." Danell's wrapped fist pumps as he coughs. "When's the big day?"

"One more month maybe."

Mike and the girls return with snacks. Mitch drinks the orange juice and breaks off a piece of candy bar. Trina returns with paperwork and mentions the bill and, if it comes to it, upcoming court fees; she and Danell can cover one but not both.

"We'll help with one," Mitch says, caramel on his chin. "You pick. We'll help."

Mike nods yes.

"Thank you," she says as Danell, dizzy, mumbles the same.

"Can we go back to the cartoon?" the girls ask.

Mitch snags the remote from Danell. Another cartoon begins. A flannel-capped hunter is convinced he can catch the same rabbit—certain now, unlike the other times when at the last minute his traps failed and the rabbit escaped, not because the traps were faulty but because the rabbit found a way. Mitch leans back in the chair next to Danell. Everyone but him watches the TV: Trina rocking her baby boy; her girls eating and drinking while watching the cartoon; Mike laughing with the girls; Danell falling asleep; the rabbit outsmarting the hunter and freeing himself. Mitch lowers his glasses and rubs his eyes.

After leaving Grandpa Ike's office, Danell and Mitch rode their bikes to the stream winding through the woods behind the house. They learned to take the shorter path through thorns, thickets, steep ledges, and in summer, ticks, black widows, and snakes. Boys waited for them on the longer path—waited more for Mitch than Danell. They carried their slurs and their whistles and kisses before bringing fists and sticks and BB guns and bats. Their line never bent into a circle surrounding Mitch and Danell; they stood across leaves and twigs, like checkers pieces, water trickling behind them, birds singing on limbs. They collapsed their line if Mitch tried running away—usually three of them and all from school, two of them from the church Danell and his parents went to; never more than three except one June when their cousins or friends came to town and Mitch saw them and told Danell. When those boys' driveways emptied, Danell said, "They're gone for the weekend. Like Grandpa and Grandma at the river. Now's our chance."

He and Danell spent all morning in the woods; returned to the house for lunch but stuffed it in their backpacks; and reached a spot deeper than they had been, overlooking a quarry they wanted to see but couldn't until that day.

Danell pulled from his backpack the rabbits matchbox and the box of firecrackers and wanted Mitch to have the first light. They jumped up and down, whooping and hollering. They dared each other to hold on as long as they could. Mitch cut down some of the wicks, and Danell never let go until the burns ended. They sang songs and timed bangs to drum beats and guitar riffs. They wondered if the universe started like that—not with God but with the Big Bang they read about. Danell blew up a small rock pile, hoping for buried gold or silver. Mitch smiled when the stream could not snuff out all the sparks he placed there. Smoke rose into summer light and a blue sky blocked out by the trees he and Danell napped under.

But bikes soon broke branches behind them. The boys catcalled and motioned to Mitch. One way out for him was through the line of boys on their bikes; the other was for Mitch and Danell to ditch their bikes and slide down the quarry and trek back home, cutting across the interstate.

The boys got off their bikes and closed in on Mitch and Danell who yanked off his shirt, tied it to a stick, lit it, and handed the flame to Mitch, whispering, "Don't let them get close to you." Shielding Mitch and lighting wicks, he charged the line, stuffing firecrackers down shirts, pants, in socks and hair—anywhere he could hold the fire long enough before pulling away his hand and facing fists and kicks, the smell of burned flesh and hair and screams rising from trees, the line breaking up and retreating, crying and pleading, Danell cut and bruised but shouting for more until his voice gave out, his fingers raw, and Mitch, behind Danell's flashes of light, not running away and no longer having the shadows of the woods follow him wherever he went.

Dioramas

Out of the butterfly room, they wander and turn the corner until the curator stops them in front of the animals. A mother clicks her stroller's brakes. Across from her, a man arrives last, floats near the back, and continues glancing at the butterflies. He wears a small sticker stamped with the American flag; the woman at the ticket office peeled it from a roll after telling him about discounted admission for military. Before meeting his tour group, he wandered the first floor and held the sticker like something delicate had landed on his fingertip, but after a man, sporting the same sticker and wearing a dark blue hat with oranges, reds, and yellows, like small wings, under the word VETERAN, shook hands, Ross smoothed the sticker across his chest when he stood alone and the group inched forward through the doors and, before circling the main display, crossed the threshold together.

In the taxidermy room, window screens block morning sun, yet the bison's polished eyes gleam. With one hoof forward, the stance remembers him as though he grazes by a stream and wind cuts across him and the square of land beneath him; his coat shines under lights; bits of plastic grass dangle from his chin. This one figure is frozen among the waxen horse; eagle and sparrows circling on strings from the ceiling; deer huddling among trees, tall grasses, and wildflowers painted in the room—

the past never emerging from where it hides until a space has been cleared for it.

The mother coos to the stroller until her baby's fussing subsides, but he cries again, and Carol fishes in her purse for a bag and places on Simon's tray grapes that, sliced narrowly, resemble samples taken from a sea. Simon oozes with joy and saliva slickens his cheeks as the grapes gush in his hands and mouth. Carol pretends to take away a grape, and Simon giggles and hums as his legs buck and his arms pump. The clanging echoes in the room; the crowd and Ross smile; the curator continues talking. Carol takes one grape from the bag and chews it and then another one—but one she missed slicing. She rattles the stroller, and Simon cries louder, face redder, his tiny head swiveling as his mother chokes. Dropping to her knees, her gray skirt spreads on the tile like feathers, while she grasps her throat and its sound of wind chasing itself through a pipe.

The crowd divides; Ross pushes his way through. He has been here before but near Kabul when an IED detonated during curfew patrol and the shrapnel sliced open Kevin, his brother-in-arms who planned on marrying his high-school sweetheart, starting a family, and irritating his dad by not inheriting his sod business and, instead, enrolling in photography classes when he returned to Virginia; and when Ross, wiping dust off Kevin as he suffocated, whispered, "Say it again. Come on, Kev. One more time. Nah-fuk. Nah-fuk," mimicking Kevin's accent and repeating their joke of embellishing the second syllable of Kevin's hometown that followed them everywhere, through desert heat and mountains and snow and shadows shifting between buildings and on streets, and every day over there.

Around Carol's waist Ross wraps his arms and pulses his fists under her sternum until the grape pops out. The curator offers to call an ambulance, but tearful, gasping, kissing her baby, Carol waves them off, repeatedly thanks the man with the sticker, and quickly departs. Under a shade tree, she texts her husband before calling him. "Did you get his name?" he asks. "We should do something for him." "No," she sobs. Her eyes follow the museums' steps and stop at the top and its two large doors.

After he's sure Carol and Simon have left, Ross exits and boards the subway. Before reaching the cemetery, he pulls into a pub, orders whiskey and a pint, and wrestles with the guilt of breaking Lent, but today has curled back to other days much further from this day, like trails of dominoes fallen in a place that has become spectral and an afterthought. The stout arrives in its frosted glass adorned with a pirate ship near a cove, the skull-and-crossbones raised high.

As a child, when he and his siblings hiked the woods, he stopped in front of a cave nowhere near buried treasure, a beach, the ocean, or gunfire. A metal gate and a padlock sealed the cave. Locals sent the terminally ill and incurably crippled there to die—

the marker bolted in the rocks saying as much. Behind the hot air, a cold darkness gripped his chest.

The Kindness of Strangers – Man Saves Choking Mother Then Vanishes blinks on the TV news. The waitress returns, offers a menu, suggests the surf-and-turf special. Ross declines and stalls paying his tab. Wanting to return to the butterfly room overwhelms other guilts. Before the group reached the dioramas, he stood among the rainbow-like wings pinned to a clear background. The curator encouraged the visitors to look closer at the pieces speaking to them. A mother and her stroller glided past the doorway. The spectrum of small things hovered in light on hidden supports and cast delicate shadows going nowhere. One pair of wings resembled sand soaking up blood. He could rearrange his return flight for later. The cemetery is a long walk down the road and will be there tomorrow, when he'll be anonymous again.

Inroads

She slides down from the fish case to the lobsters curled like question marks her happiness for tonight answers. The monger finishes wrapping Sadeeyah's tilapia, divvies the lobsters, and places her orders on the scale before ringing her up. She hands the man cash, telling him to keep the rest; chimes, "See you soon"; and shoulders her kente bag before leaving the market for the bus that takes her to a stop near a flower hedge until it fades blocks over at the walkway cutting around the sculpture rising in the garden bordered by concrete walls behind the museum. She opens the door labeled CUSTODIAL and stuffs her jacket on the shelf and her groceries alongside Rose's sack lunch in the small refrigerator—spaces Rose had to herself but, after Sadeeyah was hired, said, "Put whatever you want there. It's yours as much as mine."

"Get something good for the two of you?"

Sadeeyah turns to Rose's voice cracking as she rolls out a bucket. "I'll make the same dish we had for our first anniversary. Tonight's our sixth."

"A trip down memory lane. I like it."

"I'm so excited." Sadeeyah logs into the computer and opens her timesheet. "We're looking forward to it. But it's a surprise." She giggles. "Don't tell him."

"I promise not to stir the nest." Rose's stenciled eyebrows flutter. "We celebrated ours with a trip to the lake."

"Oh, I've heard so much about it." She scrolls through work email. "We haven't been yet. Tony promised a trip. Maybe this summer."

"You can see stars away from all the traffic that's now here. All those people from other cities." Rose lines up boxes of latex gloves and masks. "I was your age when that was then. Long before you and Tony. Right around the time Carl's dad died, and we had to do something about the farm. It wasn't for us and not for him anymore. But that company had no problem buying us out."

"Did you walk away from it with some money?"

"Shoot. Only enough to pay off his debts and the funeral. And the rest to set a wish upon."

Sadeeyah pauses on a request. "Ms. Nesbin wants to see me this morning. I hope it's nothing bad."

"You-know-who up there probably complaining about us." Rose snaps a mask snaps across her wrinkles and wiry hair. Her voice gravels. She turns on the ventilator—back walls shake, ceiling creaks, refrigerator shimmies.

Sadeeyah tightens her headscarf, pulls on a mask and gloves, and pours cleaning agents into the bucket as the computer blinks 9:30 AM. Their cart rumbles across pavement and under the overhang between custodial and the museum's back entrance.

Rose swipes her fob across the scanner, and they enter the double doors wide enough for more than art to pass through and bright enough to frame anyone standing there or coming and going.

The ground-floor elevator dings, and as Rose steps in, Sadeeyah turns for the offices.

"I should see her first."

"You could help me then come down. She ain't going nowhere."

"I hope it'll be quick. I'll be right up." Before Sadeeyah knocks on the office door and the elevator closes, she glances at Rose glaring into the space her mop's rusted and chipped handle divides the offices from her.

"Good morning, Sadeeyah. Have a seat, please." Nesbin motions to the chair by her desk. "I want to talk to you about the children's room. Who takes care of it?"

"It was Rose and I when I started, but now it's her."

"And only her now?"

"Yes."

"How does that work?"

"We start on the top floors and make our way down. When we reach the mezzanine, I clean the gallery with those TVs and tubes, and she'll go to the other half."

"Did she tell you to do that?"

"She said, 'I'll take this. You go over there.'"

"When did she say that?"

Sadeeyah looks from Nesbin's long row of office windows and toward the garden's concrete walls blocked like a labyrinth where, after fall started, Rose and a woman Sadeeyah had seen around the museum yelled at each other—the woman jabbing at Rose who clutched her duster and shook her head while turning away as the treetops blazed no exit for either woman. Crying, Rose told Sadeeyah about the altercation. "I'm not sure," Sadeeyah replies. "Before the start of the new year."

"And she does this every day?"

"Yes."

"We have concerns about missing art supplies. Do you know anything about that?"

Sadeeyah shifts in her seat and rolls in her lips; her hands clench in her lap. "No."

"Would you be willing to clean it?"

"Without Rose?"

"Please." Nesbin's pupils sharpen the ice blue in her jacket and push-pull Sadeeyah.

"Um…OK."

"And let me know if anything seems out of place after you take over."

Sadeeyah hums an incomplete yes.

"Great." Nesbin reaches out. "Thank you."

Sadeeyah shakes the director's hand, but before she leaves, she pivots. "She's my supervisor. I'm doing what she told me."

"I know."

The office door clicks closed behind her, and Sadeeyah pushes the up arrow but, after the elevator arrives, walks the stairs and seeks shadows where, pausing before she reaches the top, she wonders what she agreed to and catches her breath but not because of the ascent.

. . .

"Elevator not working?" the guard asks, leaning from a closet.

Sadeeyah stops staring at Rose mopping in one of the main gallery's corners. "I wanted some exercise."

Hank chuckles. "I'd rather be outside doing that on a day like this." He clicks open a panel; flips switches; and steps out and waves until the camera outside the closet blinks on its red light, as does one on the opposite wall, above charcoal studies of hands interlocking, pulling ropes, and gripping hilts. He then double-locks doors and strides from the main gallery and its four corners glowing faint halos under their cameras.

Exhibition pieces subdue the sounds of Sadeeyah's shoes as she plods in, but spaces between vitrines and cases hold the echoes of her long, slow entrance and her long shadow stopping short of reaching Rose. She passes painted grass or rock paths cutting through forests; along rivers; up to mountains where sunlight strengthens or surrenders to the night; or paths twisting among charred landscapes or shapes tinted as brightly as advertisements, stores, and restaurants that swirled around her when she landed in America. She passes scrolls of fading continents, broken shorelines, and unfinished interiors and a stand holding goggles and its screens flickering future places. Signs shaping a suburban house foreground a sprawling photo of public housing: DEAD END and NO EXIT hang like lanterns. And she pauses between the cleaning-supplies cart, CAUTION WET FLOOR signs, Rose stepping back, and the exhibition's focus: newspaper scraps forming a world map where Sadeeyah paused after its installation at the start of the year and showed Rose the village in Africa from where she and Tony fled. "I'm glad you got here in one piece," Rose said that day before offering help from her church—"small congregation but everyone's got big hearts." Sadeeyah thanked her and told her another church had arranged everything, including housing for Tony and her and the museum job.

"They kept you a long time." Rose returns to the bucket in the back third of the floor she hasn't laced soap and water across. "You get lost?"

"No," Sadeeyah's voice quivers.

"They got you all sweaty."

Sadeeyah forces a smile as she pats her cheeks. "It's so warm today. Hank said to me he'd rather be outside walking."

"He's a walker this time of year." Rose wrings out her mop. "What'd they say?"

"She want us to improve some areas." Sadeeyah grabs a bottle and rags from under the cart. "She wants the two of us to improve some areas."

"You new here again?" Rose giggles. "Those are the dirty ones."

Grimacing, Sadeeyah finds the fresh rags.

"What else?"

"She want us to not split up."

"No… Divide and conquer." Rose thrusts her mop. "That's how we've been doing it."

"She thinks we'll be better off if we do things together. Like we did when I started."

"But you got all this down now on your own. I trained you." Rose's jaw tenses. "They need to tell me before telling you. I'm not saying you can't know and pass it on to me, but they need to be forthright." She cuts across Sadeeyah for the cart. "Anything else from them?"

"No."

"No 'Thank you' or 'Keep up the good work'?"

"She thanks us."

Rose finishes a lane, rolls the cart down to the other third, mops a section like a storm shredding fabric, and reviews where she was, spot-checking near Sadeeyah. "Which areas? Their offices? Hers? They want us to go to their houses and clean them too?"

Her neck and forehead reheating, Sadeeyah dusts baseboards quicker. "On the mezzanine."

"You show me exactly where they said."

The elevator delivers Sadeeyah and Rose to the mezzanine, and Hank welcomes them with a good morning and hums a song while walking to rooms near smaller galleries.

"Mornin'," Rose mutters, pausing to sip from her coffee wedged between pipe cleaners and polish.

The cart clangs as Sadeeyah pushes it behind Rose and her bucket and locks its wheels between the galleries, the rooms, and the staircase leading to the ground floor. She loads supplies into a handcart and, after Rose disappears around a corner, where her mop slaps and sloshes, darts for the middle room labeled CHILDREN AND FAMILY PROGRAMS. Sadeeyah closes the door and dusts shelves, crayons, pencils, markers, brushes, and paints; inspects rolls of papers; wipes down tables and chairs; and empties trash cans, pausing at the dented one Rose kicked after she found a drawing of a skinny woman topped with wild red hair and eyebrows inked like a clown's.

The door creaks open.

"OK, it's you," Hank says, waving to Sadeeyah. "No, we're good," he speaks into his walkie-talkie. His shoes thunder away.

Sadeeyah moves for the door, but Rose appears.

"You cleaning here?"

"I was over here and wanted to knock it out. I'll do the others while I'm here."

Rose scans the room. "I'll see you down at the offices."

Sadeeyah calms herself and exits the room, passing behind Hank standing under a camera and waving until its light turns on.

Nesbin's office is empty when Sadeeyah meets Rose outside it. They plug in the vacuum and tidy up, careful not to disturb papers and folders or bump the computer and the surge protector. They finish the ground-floor offices before the museum opens and the children's programs start.

Rose lights a cigarette and, slouching in the parking lot, takes a long drag. "I want to apologize for earlier."

"It's OK."

"I can't go much more with them." Rose's ashes drift into the smell of honeysuckle. "You and I do this, and we'll do it their way. Thanks for telling me."

Sadeeyah leans agains the brick separating the large access doors from custodial where, from inside, she heard the woman who had confronted Rose in the garden call her "white trash" to another woman as their dresses sashayed and heels clacked before they entered the museum.

Rose takes another long drag. Smoke curls out of her. "They're above me. Even though I've been here longer. But they came to you because you're a good employee."

"That's because you trained me."

"We make a good team." Rose snuffs the cigarette on the brick. "Let's finish up and get some lunch."

"And some tea."

"I loved what we had last time."

"Oh, it's my favorite, Rose."

"It was real good."

"And it's from where I'm from."

"I remember you said that!"

They unload their cart and prop their door open as the ventilator rumbles out fumes.

. . .

After her "Hi…Tony?" to their small apartment returns no response, Sadeeyah cleans up—the chemical smells of her day, burned between Rose and colleagues, linger—digs through cabinets, and checks her phone for Tony saying he's left work. The tilapia simmers when she pours in coconut milk and mangoes and shakes in turmeric. She starts rice, dices tomatoes, and snaps coriander sprigs for the lobsters she keeps in their shells, like her family did. She clicks on the news, sets the table, and finds the candles she made for the church's fundraiser for medical and missionary supplies. She pats the long scar running from the dent between her earlobe and jaw and across her collarbone when a report comes on about attacks and kidnappings spiking and a new faction marching into villages around her hometown. A Red Cross spokesperson discusses aid insurgents contaminated and requests more as children swell in the background. The front door unlocks, Tony smiles on his way in, and the journalist describes helicopters hovering over men playing soccer within fields marked by camouflaged squads and guns slung on their hips.

"Good evening, sweetie." He kisses her. "Smells good. Give me a minute to change," he says, walking to the bedroom.

"You didn't give me a heads-up."

"Do you have something for me? Want to come here and show me in the sheets?"

"Tonight. After dinner." Blushing, she signs the card she hid in a drawer:

> Every day I thank God we found our way out together and someone found us after we asked God to help us get here where we celebrate our new life and anniversary.

She lights the candles, double-checks the table, and cuts up Tony's portions. The news releases her when it switches to music and Tony peeks around the corner.

"Close your eyes," he says.

Glass thumps on the linoleum, and wrapping rustles.

"Open them."

The overhead lights and sunset silhouette Tony's first nice shirt he found at the thrift store a month after they settled, the sleeve Sadeeyah stitched up the bicep, and the arm cocked behind his back matching the other amputated at the elbow. His left arm offers a card tied to a flower bouquet, and stepping to the side, he reveals a bottle of wine.

"Happy anniversary."

"Thank you." She dabs her eyes after reading and reminiscing that Tony's handwriting with his other hand has improved since they've been married—through smoke and shrapnel and bullets and debris; the two of them separated but never for long.

Unfolding a napkin in his lap, he beams over the dishes. "This is familiar."

"I hope it tastes as good as the first time."

"It'll be better in many ways."

They bless their food and ask for protection for their family and friends abroad and close by—"and guidance" Sadeeyah adds.

Tony's small chest rises and falls after his tastes the fish and yams. "Delicious."

"How was work?"

"That couple I told you about won't meet in the middle. The seller's willing to provide credit for a new roof, but they don't want that. And who wouldn't want a new roof over them?" His head wags, but his milky eye stays on his plate.

"Stubborn."

"Like weeds. And when they get together, nothing else grows." He pours two glasses of wine and slides one toward Sadeeyah. "How was yours?"

Sadeeyah exhales as she cracks open the lobsters and scrapes out meat. "I took over cleaning the children's room. Ms. Nesbin asked me to."

"Rose is still having trouble?"

"They think she's stealing art supplies now."

"They should've stopped this."

"She wants me to spy on her. Report back." Sadeeyah ladles the red sauce. "I don't want to tattle."

"It shouldn't be you."

"She's been good to me. And they're both my bosses."

"We can't have you involved that way. You can't help the wrong person at the wrong time and place." He chews and swallows. "One of the condos will be available soon. The one by the market."

She looks at him.

"First floor. Good space. We can get out of here…and start our family." He stabs a lobster chunk. "You can walk out the front door for groceries. And walk back before I take you to work. Your food doesn't have to sit in that tiny fridge all day."

"What about the bus?"

"I'll be closer to the office. I'll drive us."

Sadeeyah beams before glancing at the shells splayed toward sunset and the hour hanging between evening and night—reds matching the shells.

"This is such a nice surprise. Thank you." He leans over the table and kisses her. "And I have a surprise for you. Pastor Evan and his family and Lisa and her sister want to take us for ice cream to celebrate with us. Save some room for dessert. Or not." He winks, dishing seconds of rice.

"You finish that." She scoots the serving bowls closer to him. "I'm having *two* scoops of ice cream because of today."

• • •

The bus drops her off, and Sadeeyah steps behind the garden's concrete walls. Under the overhang between the back entrance and custodial, Rose and the children's director yell—not loud but rigid. Gosner's slim finger stabs about. As Gosner's tone rises and her stabbing intensifies, Rose presses the mop handle into her chest, covering her heart.

"You're using too many chemicals in there. We've been over this before. We have kids in there. And parents. And I've asked you to change what you use. We smell it every time. It's literally debilitating." Bracelets rattle down Gosner's arm as she mimes suffocation and gagging. "Why haven't you switched?"

"Costs too much."

"I'm willing to pay for the same products I use. I told you that last month."

Sadeeyah tightens her headscarf and walks—shoulders back; chin up; eyes forward—toward custodial.

"Ma'am, I have to put in a request to Ms. Nesbin and Mr. Michio about the next fiscal year."

"Why haven't you?"

"I just haven't."

"Good morning," Sadeeyah says louder than usual. "Excuse me." She proceeds between the two women and sets on the desk a bag of apples and her lunch; pretends her personal effects are stored there—all over and under the desk; and lingers between Rose and Gosner: a cough, a hum, rummaging in her bag, opening the fridge, rolling a bucket and supplies toward the threshold, opening and closing desk drawers. She sits in the chair and scrolls through websites she does not care about.

"Get to it." Gosner glances at Sadeeyah's hard typing. "*Please.*" She checks herself. "I know you work hard here. We all do. We've all been stressed over the opening. And I know budgets are tight. I'll talk to Robert about freeing some money." She grabs her coffee off the windowsill and struts into the museum and toward the offices.

Sniffling, Rose cycles between tense, calm, sadness. "Her lily-white face can kiss my lily-white butt." She spits on the ground before her forefinger, stained from nicotine, taps up her nose. "Hoity-toity horse shit."

"What happened?"

"I get here, same time every day, and here she is." Rose lights a cigarette. "And she follows me right here. She says, 'I noticed our room still smells.' And she kept on from there."

"I'm sorry."

"Worst one yet." She snubs her smoke and helps Sadeeyah load the cart as the ventilator kicks on.

Sadeeyah puts away her jacket, lunch, and bag, save for one apple she washes in the sink. She flicks water off and offers the apple to Rose who crunches a big bite after saying thank you and motions if Sadeeyah wants a bite.

"That's all yours."

"Makes my morning better."

They gather their gear and enter the back door. The elevator arrives, and they start on the top floor and work their way down to the mezzanine.

"Yuck. What a mess," Rose says. "All those cobwebs. How'd we miss those?"

Sadeeyah looks where Rose's chin motions toward the corner topped by the camera on the wall opposite the children's room. She squints at glints, mismatched and chipped paint, and repaired plaster.

"Help me get up there." Rose grabs a cloth and spray can.

They position the ladder until it doesn't block the children's room. Rose leans on the first step; her left leg stiffens and hiccups the higher she climbs. Sadeeyah presses her weight toward the floor, steadying the ladder as Rose wiggles her frail body and arm behind the camera and swats her cloth around the lens.

Snickering and talking rise and fall in the children's room.

"Hand me that can," Rose says.

Sadeeyah balances on the ladder while reaching for the cart. Climbing steps, she meets Rose's arm halfway. The ladder shakes when Rose shakes the can. Foam bubbles over the lens. The power-on light fades red to pink to gray as the cloud covers the glass and drips onto the wires.

Laughter and claps burst from the children's room.

"Shoot."

"What is it?" Sadeeyah asks.

"I think I got some inside. Hank won't be too happy about that." Rose dabs the camera. "Is he here?"

Sadeeyah turns toward the main entrance and security desk. "I can't tell."

"I bet he's out walking."

Chairs screech in the children's room. A woman leaves for the bathroom and quiets when she passes the ladder, Rose, and Sadeeyah. The door behind her does not close.

Rose unplugs the camera. "Better safe than sorry. Bo got all shocked up when he was in the Air Force. He was working on an engine, and someone forgot to give him a heads-up. Would you get one of those thicker pipe cleaners we have? That should do it."

Sadeeyah pushes items in the cart. "They must be in the shop. I'll be back."

"I'll be here." Rose's head lowers as the noise in the children's room swells and recedes.

On her tiptoes, at the back of custodial, Sadeeyah finds a bundle of long pipe cleaners, and when she returns to the ladder, Rose is not on it. The children's room door remains open, and Sadeeyah peers in. The woman who left for the bathroom and another woman huddle in the corner, their hands covering their shock. Purple goo oozes down Gosner's skirt and desk as Rose seethes, holstering a jug, and yells, "If you don't want me to hear you talking about me, close your damn door next time!"

. . .

Sadeeyah signs the invoice for the new month's supplies, and the delivery truck rumbles out of the parking lot. She rolls a dolly under the pallet, pumping it twice before wheeling it inside custodial where she organizes shelves for the new and types on the computer which of the old need pickup and disposal—a task Rose started training Sadeeyah for. While she handled the delivery, an email arrived, and Tony left a voicemail. *I have a surprise for us. How does the lake tonight sound? Don told me Friday nights in May don't have many people and the sunsets are amazing. We'll have a picnic. I'll come by the museum. See you after five.* She checks the time and can't wait to clock out but retreats when Nesbin's email asks her to stop by before leaving for the day.

She knocks on the office door but shies behind the frame as Nesbin bobs a teabag in a mug. "You wanted to see me?"

"Yes. Hi there. Come in."

Sadeeyah pulls out the chair.

Nesbin brushes her off. "No. This won't take long. I wanted to thank you for taking on the extra duties for the interim. It's been a lot these few weeks, but you've done a tremendous job."

"Thank you."

"And I also wanted to let you know it should be another week or so."

Sadeeyah finds her way through Nesbin's voice. "And that's when Rose will be back?"

"HR may send you someone. I know Meredith Gosner and her team appreciate you taking on more, especially as our summer camps start." Nesbin sips. "Any plans for the weekend?"

"My husband and I are going to the lake tonight. He's on his way."

"That's wonderful. Don't let me keep you."

"It's a great place to see stars."

"I didn't know that. Well, have a great time and thanks again. See you Monday." The world map on Nesbin's mug tilts back and flattens as though anyone could cross multiple places without resistance.

When Sadeeyah reaches custodial, Tony pulls into the lot and idles near the garden entrance where during breaks Rose and Sadeeyah chatted and wound the paths in the warm seasons—among flowers, grasses, sunlight—or in winter where they left footprints in snow as cold as the concrete walls bordering them. But when rain fell, they stood under the overhang, talked, and watched water slant across the parking lot. Sadeeyah returns Tony's wave when he holds up a to-go bag from their favorite sandwich shop. She grabs her sack from the fridge and her jacket from the shelf from where a drawing, signed by children and Gosner and her staff, falls onto the floor. THANK YOU FOR CLEANING OUR ROOM the rainbow puffy letters say above a dark-skinned woman donning a headscarf and holding a broom and surrounded by art. After someone slipped it onto the shelf when Sadeeyah was at lunch, she has yet to hang it in the shop or take it home.

Tony's opens the passenger door. "Hi there, sweetie. Ready?"

"Hang on."

Sadeeyah returns to the offices. "Ms. Nesbin?"

"Yes?" She stops working on a catalogue.

"No one has said anything to me about what happened with Rose. Or why it did happen."

"Do you want me to have someone from HR contact you?"

"Do you know what they say about her?"

"Who?"

Sadeeyah pulls out the chair and sits down.

All Clear

Hazards flashing, the truck stops, and a stringy man slides from the passenger side and staggers to wildflowers speckling the ditch. He clenches before dry-heaving as wind picks up and the diesel rumbles under thunder, cool air, and dark clouds graying out the blue horizon.

"Lunch talking back to you?"

"The doctors need to adjust some things." Ron ignores Gerry's help as he struggles back into the cab.

Gerry reaches into the cooler behind his seat and hands a water bottle to Ron who takes it and quickly turns the radio up, but the meteorologist's update breaks up the song: storm cells in neighboring counties have merged and, if the squall stays its course, will line the land leading to the mountains.

"Damn," Ron rasps. He sips and wipes his sweat.

"The weather? Or…?"

"The weather," Ron snaps.

Gerry slicks back his receding hair, settles his ball cap, and shifts into the truck into gear. Static cuts up the next song scratching from the speakers. The twin mufflers reverberate under the Cherokee Nation license plate and 9/11 NEVER FORGET and International Association of Fire Fighters stickers on the fender. The country singer sings killing time is killing him while the truck heads deeper into the woodlands thickening along the slopes and crags of the Ouachitas.

"Afternoon," the ranger says at a gate closing off the park. "We're asking new arrivals to hold off from setting up camp until the storms pass."

"Except for them." Ron nods to tents and vehicles gathering along the main road inside the campground.

"We're asking them to be accommodating."

"When did you do that?"

The ranger demurs.

"What do you suggest?" Gerry asks.

"Going to any of the towns around here."

Chuckling, Ron leans in. "Because the storms will just up and skip over them?"

"Should only be a few hours after which you can enjoy your stay."

Gerry looks at Ron who shakes his head in a lopsided yes. "Would you let us check in early?"

"Yes, sir. We can do that."

"Great. Thank you so much."

"Name?"

"Gerry Hummingbird."

The ranger scans his printout, punches a hole in a parking pass, and hands it to Gerry who reverses his truck into a shelter area. The cold disappears after he rolls up his window. Drizzle dissipates clouds, but the clouds gather again.

"All those fish will have to wait for us a little longer," Gerry says. "But it'll be worth it."

"Bigfoot too."

"Let's hope for your sake, he doesn't have a buffet before we get to them."

"But that's when I catch him. He'll be enjoying his fish and never see me coming." Ron sticks out his right hand, sewn together at the second knuckle blending into his palm, where broken glass had snagged him ascending a building when its ceiling tile blinded him after it crashed on his helmet; he closes his right hand around his left striding like a primate. He holds this scene until the drizzle hardens into rain and slaps the truck.

"You're on your own for that." Gerry's laugh subsides. "I got to be elsewhere now."

"Old age has put you elsewhere."

"Welcome to the club, brother."

Ron scrounges for beer in the cooler.

Gerry glimpses the prescription bottle Ron tossed on the floorboard. "Let's get to town. If a tornado comes, I want something sweet in my tummy. Best way to hunker down for a bit. Now where you going?"

After Ron slips out, he heads for a port-a-potty underneath the shelter where two tethered Irish setters wander from a cut-through in brush surrounding the ranger station and parking lot. When a young boy and girl appear from the woods and herd the dogs, Ron pauses returning to the truck before they vanish. A woman arrives, and Gerry watches her open her arms and coax the children and dogs while the air teeters between holding its lull or pulling apart the land and the paths through it.

. . .

They grab two seats at the counter. Gerry winks at the waitress who, grinning, answers his questions about the menu. The dessert case twirls behind her, and Gerry's eyes chase the last slice of red velvet cake. The waitress motions for a scoop of ice cream, and agreeing, Gerry broadens his gut and leans back on his stool, which he soon retreats from when the slim back supports him less than his truck's extra cushion. Ron chats with locals while skimming the morning's paper and rummaging through tourist guides; a map highlighting the town's main streets, restaurants, shops, and attractions; coupons from the downtown business association; and an alternative-health directory where he pauses on accessing past lives.

"They got a museum." Ron slaps a page.

Gerry chews while he leans toward Ron but pulls away when the waitress bobs her eyebrows from behind the kitchen. Crimson spreads across Gerry's lips and teeth when he smiles.

"One of those shows was out here for it during that conference they have every year. They were telling me about it." Ron thumbs toward the elderly couple who sat next to him and, on their way out, offered their seats to college students dressed for hiking. A sorority sister alongside Ron drags her finger across a game flashing on her phone: A figure rises into a sky where other figures, dragged and locked there, chain each other; the figures waiting on the ground roam alone, bump into objects, fall into pits, and loop their arms into anything that can catch them. "Christ…I forgot it already. I used to watch it. What was it?" He knuckles his forehead.

"It'll come back to you."

"I'll have to check it out while we're doing nothing else here." He tears the page out.

The waitress cruises by.

Gerry says, "I'm staying right here for a while."

Ron's alarm beeps.

Gerry stares at the prescription bottle Ron doesn't open and stuffs back into his pocket. "You should too. It'd be good for you."

"Ask your lady friend to pour a little Jack in here for me." Ron raises his coffee cup at the waitress and spins around when she tends to a family of six in ponchos sitting at the table behind him.

"I don't think that'll help."

"Sheila ask you to mother-hen me all weekend?"

Gerry wipes his mouth and stirs his Coke.

"I'll be outside." Ron shoots up and tosses his napkin on his seat. He pays the bill at the front of the diner where shapes in the windows connect, disconnect, reconnect.

As Gerry turns Ron's way, the woman from the campground ties her two dogs to a post; her children wiggle in front of her. She points to the spot under her sandals; pulses three fingers while mouthing *Three o'clock*; and hands money to the boy. The blue sky splits a little more; clouds close in but do not reach the town. The woman starts to speak, qualifying something, but her kids cut her off and scamper down Main Street and nearly trip over Ron resting against a wall and massaging his neck before he drifts down storefronts and side streets.

The woman enters the diner and asks for water for her dogs resting under the overhang. The waitress drops ice cubes into a dish for the woman who thanks her and peeks at Gerry nursing his cake and drink. The softness of the woman's face; the slim shape of her; her hair like fields curling around sunlight: he knows her but from years ago as another woman whom he kept everything about her and the places they met secret from his wife.

The pain from sitting too long spirals along his ribs, hips, and knees. On his way outside, he leaves a large tip for the waitress. He clicks his tongue at the dogs flopped over. Their ears perk, and they wag their tails as they peer up before returning to lapping their water. The woman turns and looks at, away from, and back to Gerry; smiling, she loops a strand of hair behind her ear—without a ring on her hand. Gerry sucks in his gut; his body sweats; his hands shake. Before speaking to her, he double-checks the street but can't find Ron.

· · ·

As the Doppler radar shrinks and grows its mass over counties, the woman behind the desk balances Ron's credit card, coupon, and ticket. A red banner flashes updates for hail, downpours of rain, potential for flash floods, high winds, and lightning strikes that shift as quickly as they arrive on screen.

"If the sirens go off, the bathroom's the safest spot." The woman points.

Ron glances down the hallway leading from the museum's lobby: to the right, an exit sign floats above a light outlining the thin gap between a door and the ground; to the left, silhouettes and sounds pulse in darkness.

"And if they don't, we may close early." She empties a coffee pot into her mug. "We got a loudspeaker. I'll let you know."

"Yes, ma'am. Thank you." Before stepping in, he checks the front window: the sky half blue, half obscured.

Among vitrines, media, and artifacts, Bigfeet huddle inside the first diorama. A female, cradling an infant as big as a sack of flour, drags a deer corpse toward flowers around bones and carcasses in a pit. The male, having stacked stones and tree limbs for a shelter alongside the river and in the woods, stands watch over the mountainside that hides his family but also cloaks surprises in the distance; his ginger back and arms spread, he towers two feet above Ron. An overhead soundtrack brings the sounds of birds, water, leaves, and wind; grunts from the adults; and chirps from children.

Ron steps from the rail. Two young Bigfeet point at the moon glowing on the ceiling at the far end of the scene. Clouds collect atop plywood panels gaping in the middle of the sky painted a thin band of blue linked to black. The lone yellow bulb illuminates patches of land like the countryside and the farm where Ron and his sister spent seasons playing in the snow; running through fields, trees, and wildflowers, singing with bullfrogs, and chasing grasshoppers and lightning bugs along the pond; and where the colors of autumn never left him: fires in the trees contrasting the grasses' greens; fires surrounded by autumn fog low on the ground like smoke; fires lasting after leaves fall and the thick and deep char they leave that a voice struggles cutting through.

He falls forward but catches himself. Too dizzy to stand, he sits on a tree-trunk bench, drops his head, and breathes faster and harder but then slower after he pops open the prescription bottle and forces down a pill. Thunder rolls over the museum. He turns in the darkness when the children from the camp giggle and scramble behind him.

* * *

"Hi. Did the park tell you to come here?"

The woman stops scratching her dogs' ears and beams up at Gerry. "They sure did. You?"

"I thought I saw you over there. I'm at the same campsite. Gerry." He squats to the dogs, but his back pain stops him midway. Hunched over as long as he can, he extends his hand to the woman, keeping his left hand and wedding ring in his pocket.

"Hi. Linda. It looks like everyone is here now."

"Where else could you be but here? There are worse ways to sit this out."

"There sure are." She removes bright bracelets from one of her forearms and, focusing on Gerry, ties her hair in braids.

"My buddy and I are here through Monday. We're celebrating his retirement."

"Oh, that's great. What did he do?"

"Firefighter."

"That's a big job."

"Thank you. Me too. But I'm not retired."

Linda smiles at Gerry while smoothing her braids.

"They had to force him out."

"That must be tough."

"They promoted me to a desk job. They asked me if I wanted to stay out in it, but I wanted to free up some space for the next round of guys. It was their time."

"Do you like it?"

"How could I not? I'm still with the department, managing a lot of good people and our responsibilities, and it keeps me close with all of them. They're always coming to me for advice on something I did."

When Linda's two kids zigzag further down Main Street, the dogs wag their tails and whine.

"First time here?" Gerry asks.

"Not camping. I haven't been to this town. Some of the others around I have. They have some of the best antiques in the area. I'd hate to bore you with the details."

"No, bore me, please. I would love to hear about antiques. What's your favorite?"

"I can talk your ear off."

"Good thing I have two." His right hand tugs his right ear.

"How about you?"

"Ron and I used to make it out here whenever we had time off from the station."

Clouds crackle in the distance. The diner's lights flicker; its door chimes quicken with each open and close.

"I need to check on my kids." Linda stands and leashes the dogs tracing her gaze down Main Street.

Gerry staggers forward. "Camping's a great way to build character."

"It is. I'm the captain, cook, and clean-up crew."

"Now that's a big job. Would you like to get a drink? Dixie's up there is a good spot."

"During or after the storm?"

"Either." Gerry blushes. "Both."

Linda loops her braids over her shoulders shining like the light Gerry saw on the hood of his truck when he returned home to his wife after she called Ron at the station and asked if he had seen Gerry or knew where he was. Earlier that day, a woman who wasn't Fran stopped by. She rubbed Gerry's biceps as she winked and tugged her blouse. Gerry strutted around her car—his body leaner then; his raven hair gelled back; his cologne so thick the assistant chief teased him that taking him on a hunting trip would warn the forest—and pretended to leave but snapped back whenever she giggled. Everyone on Gerry's shift ignored these open-air meetings and his longer lunches and sick days, except for Ron who, when they were alone, asked, "Where you goin' with all this?" Ron hugged him, told him he loved him, only wanted the best. Ron's voice echoed in Gerry but not as a question.

"I don't want any confusion," Linda says. "Maybe some other time."

Linda, dogs tugging her, briskly walks toward where her kids crossed the street: a sidewalk sign carved as a Sasquatch foot.

Gerry looks that way, and the swagger, which moved him around, like heat roping up, releases him—his chest deflating; gut sliding over his belt—and drops him into a chill.

● ● ●

The kids scrabble around the museum. When the sister hides from the brother, Ron stumbles off the bench and crawls toward her to tell her to show herself—that hiding too long, never emerging when called upon, or never offering a clue won't matter because he's looking for her with more than his eyes. Deeper into dioramas, the children cross shadows and circle the lake, trees, and Bigfoot family. A flame crackles in its papier mâché; the female tightens their children. Linda's daughter crouches in a dark hollow behind that scene; her brother soon follows but, finding nothing, continues on until he disappears.

Turning toward the girl hiding next to the fire, Ron cringes as he believes the fire spills from its pit and spreads across the forest floor that falls apart beneath linoleum tile. And he sees in his vision his sister sleeping in the bedroom around the kitchen's corner where he fixed a table Rebecca bought from a secondhand store near campus after a long day split between classes and her part-time job as a hospital orderly. He drove back that October night and, home in Tulsa, drank a beer, legs propped and tired from an earlier gym workout, and watched TV. The single flame transforms in front of Ron, as it doubled back then when he was away, melting wood, plastic, and insulation after maintenance failed securing the gas line in Rebecca's apartment; Ron sees the colors triple, quadruple, and cover her carpet, furniture, and walls like autumn.

Ron lunges forward as the girl emerges; her brother, sneaking up behind her, taps her shoulder; holding hands, they squeal and scamper out of the museum.

A silhouette slides from the fiberglass forest close to the lake shimmering from a projector placed on the side. "Get on my back," it says to Ron. "I'll take you across the water."

Sweating, Ron crouches. "I'm too heavy."

The sounds of birds, frogs, and deer fade from the scene as the fire dims behind them and Ron. The silhouette moves closer to the grass between the woods and water.

"Get on my back. I'll take us."

"We'll drown halfway."

"I'll take us."

"I'm too heavy."

"You need to come in."

"I know."

"So, then…"

"I'll sink us."

"I'll take us."

"What can't I take us?" Ron asks.

The silhouette slips away. And Ron reaches for neither the water nor the fire because nothing else breaches the past or the present; the future for Rebecca remains as it began when she was rescued, after Ron nearly lost her: bound to a wheelchair, oxygen tanks, stares, pity—but thankful for the next day to arrive.

A hand lands on Ron's shoulder.

"There you are."

Ron wipes his eyes as he did whenever Gerry drove him to Fayetteville for Rebecca's therapy.

"We can go," Gerry says.

"Are the sirens going off?"

"No. The storms have gone on their way."

Gerry slings Ron up from the floor and pats his chest. Ron nods and buries his face in Gerry's embrace.

The museum employee turns the corner and walks her flashlight beam toward a black wall. All the scenes brighten after a clank and a buzz from she pulls on a box inside a closet. Further back, alongside paintbrushes, glue, plexiglass, tools, and drop cloths, two wire skeletons pose—large feet and tall frames frozen amid landscapes not yet set in place and before flesh covers them all.

Sunlight breaks through the sky, the outside air warms both men, and the squall of dark clouds burn up the farther east they push. People weave in and out of stores, down Main Street, and along streets until they break apart and wander by themselves or find their groups. Ron rests against a door; Gerry hands him a water bottle and tells him to take his time. Ahead of them, Linda, her kids, and dogs pile into her station wagon and drive away.

. . .

Gerry's truck stops at the gate's wet chain down and caked in mud.

"Welcome back," says the ranger who greeted them earlier. He points beyond trees on the left peeling off the long main road. "Our office closes here in a few minutes, but we'll open tomorrow morning at six."

Eying the ranger, Ron says, "How's the fishin' been?"

"Real good so far."

"Baby deer causing trouble yet?"

"Lots of them."

"Any Bigfoot?"

The ranger smiles like a devil. "I haven't seen any, but my colleagues say they have. I'm also new here."

Ron returns a similar smile. "You don't say."

"Thank you." Gerry puts the truck in gear.

"That explains 'bout everything now." Ron chuckles until he coughs. He reaches for the cooler and offers the first of two beers he opens. "Second time's a charm."

"I've been waiting all day for this." Gerry clinks his bottle to Ron's and takes a long swig as gravel and dirt, flowers, and greens surround the bend near Linda's station wagon, a family-sized tent, and her dogs leaping into the brush by the creek. They bounce, sniff roots and dirt, and ears up, search again for where Linda calls them from. And Gerry keeps the truck's pace—neither slowing down nor speeding up as it passes Linda, emerging from the brush, crouching, and greeting the Irish setters jogging over one at a time like blood chasing blood; her kids catch up and giggle. The truck's rearview and side mirrors and back window frame Linda and her kids as the road continues and the landscape falls backward and as Gerry, the steering wheel steady in his hands, shifts from their silhouettes to up ahead while he tastes cherry and wheat and while Linda calling the names of her dogs —Lucky and Chance—retreats into the spreading dusk.

Ron leans back, and after he drifts asleep, water edges toward him like clear paint, and he flinches as he dreams standing waist-deep in and then walking across the water and into black smoke billowing off the horizon where a capsized boat has cast its passengers who thrash about waves and struggle floating on the hull and broken mast. Were he younger, he would run into it all, not fearing what could happen to him diving into the unknown and pulling strangers into daylight. But standing there, he is neither old nor young, and he can no more run into it than from it. If he runs into it, his courage, having briefly exceeded his body, would snap back to the boundaries of bones and muscle; if he stays put, his surviving days would remind him what he could have done but did not. "Here," he mutters, twitching.

Gerry glances over but keeps driving.

One of the boat's figures swims across the water and onto a shore; the other figures soon arrive farther down. Ron starts forward, but the figure motions him to stay and, before the figure's family finds it, whispers something to Ron, its voice carrying solace.

Branches scrape the truck's doors; debris kicks back and into its underbelly; brakes squeak. Ron wakes as Gerry pops out. They unpack and talk about who's going to do the dishes, what to eat and drink for dinner and dessert, the weather the last time they were here, and what they'll see under the stars until they and the stars clear out and make space for the next day.

Creek on the Right

All but one of the horses stand in the stable. Shielding the fireplace's glow, Tom double-checks the window. Often in winter light and in sightlines from the living room to the pasture, the palomino can disappear. He places the roll of duct tape on the box marked BOOKS and steps onto the front porch. A head or rump silhouettes stalls one, two, and four; the two brownies' breaths curl in the air. Tom moves closer. The smoke-gray quarter horse has slipped out.

"He still has a basket of fruit," R.J. says, opening the door, his boots clomping from the kitchen, blue rag by his hip turned black. Flecks of food grease his jeans. "Hasn't spoiled." The rhythm of him tossing an apple counters the silence of the emptied house.

"We're missing Gunny." Tom throws his chin at the gate popped open under the moon. "I thought I locked it. I know I had my gloves on."

"Those slick Guccis you still wear?" R.J. grins while tightening his hoodie until his beard bushes out.

Tom demurs, grabs flashlights and apples, and follows his brother to the halters. "Dad's horse," he chuckles on their way to the trail.

Sleet on the ground deepens the darkness as they stumble through the woods. Neither flashlight reveals hoof tracks stamped in the middle or tumbled off into thicker brush and sinkholes. The rope dangles over the creek where they crossed when they were kids and where they now help each other over icy rocks.

Tom searches the water and moonlight and listens for more than owls. Far from that water's edge he hugged his father and brother goodbye before he went away. When Richard Sr. neared his end, the state granted Tom a one-day visit. The warden's approval, paperwork, and the drive to the hospital ate most of the day. The prison van idled in Atlanta traffic, ribboned through counties, and stopped for a guard to use the bathroom at a rest stop where the summer sun backlit the wires crisscrossing the van's windows.

They spin around as leaves crunch behind them—a large trunk snapped at its roots like dark wings too frozen to fly.

Farther on and then off the trail, limbs and frost crackling, R.J. says, "We already cut through here."

"No. The creek's on our right."

A gust shakes the woods and water.

"Come on out, Gunpowder!" R.J. shivers. "We know you're cold and hungry like us."

Tom trips on a root; his light exposes a jagged rock shimmering in sleet. He stands, blood seeping through his pants, and moves closer to the space in the distance. The bolt of blackness stretches between branches and silence and the moving of things seen and unseen. Panting, favoring his leg, he braces as if he could catch a shadow that has enough left in its core to reach him. His temptations lie elsewhere in the past but have come with him to each sliver of a new opening—not to keep them but to scatter them and step through their traces. He pulls an apple from his pocket and crunches it, his mouth wide open, exaggerating his slobbering and clicking tongue. "Too bad Gunny's not here to enjoy this. Red delicious too. His favorite." He offers a bite to R.J. who chomps down.

"Tell me about it. This would hold me over until that big ol' breakfast of oats and barley." R.J. eyes water from the cold. "Might even fart a bit from all this joy. Give Tom's horse a real stinker…that pretty palomino."

The brothers laugh.

Leaves shift in the distance.

Talking and crunching, they pass the apple back and forth; twigs snap closer.

A horse head appears before them like black satin pulled from night, the soft neck stretching toward familiar shadows.

Shaking, Tom takes the halter from R.J. and shuffles closer.

The horse jerks back and neighs.

"Easy," Tom coos.

Gunpowder rocks forward and slumps down; his eyes bulge.

"He's stuck."

The brothers dig out the horse from mud and brush and unsnag his blanket from branches as he whinnies and shakes sleet from his mane.

On the path toward the stable, R.J. flicks the gate and its rusted, crooked pin. "We can tackle this tomorrow after a lot of coffee and whiskey."

"Egg-and-sausage sandwiches from Lulu's sound good." Tom yawns and loosens his scarf.

"Speaking of, when I was cleaning out the kitchen, I found some of your letters." R.J. pops the top on a tobacco can. "Do you want them?"

Tom rubs Gunpowder's muzzle as the horse finishes a fresh apple. "Did he read them?'

"Every single one. And when he couldn't, I read them to him." R.J. offers the can.

Tom takes a pinch as they settle Gunpowder among the other horses whinnying after their sleep is disturbed. "Damn." He chokes as he takes off his gloves and fishes out the wet wad. He flicks it, steaming, to the ground. "It's been a while."

R.J. pats the smoked-colored horse, stretches his arms in a V, and trudges to the house near the patch of garden that holds their parents' ashes.

Tom extends his hands under Gunpowder's nose; the horse's warmth slides between Tom's fingers, around and under him, where he stands and where he stood.

Moonflowers

If he could plant flowers on the moon for her, he would—lilacs in craters' shadows, roses in grayscale cracks, and daisies (among her favorites) facing the long, rough edge fading into space, their yellows and oranges spiraling in black; and if he could spell her name on that same surface, he would and would time the sun's passing that brightens the petals-as-letters. But he rolls over and sniffles at the spaceships he built and strung over his bed alongside the aluminum foil–ball planets he painted. Cutting through the curtains, light reduces the small stars on the wallpaper that glowed green throughout the night and intensifies the poster of lunar phases above a calendar highlighting tomorrow and TASHA scribbled in the middle of a red circle.

His mom opens his door. "Lucas, honey, do you want to get up? It's almost noon."

He tightens the bedspread over him.

"I thought we could get out. How about Corn Dog Palace, or a float from Sims?"

The face under the bedspread's dashed-line orbits rotates left and right.

"The spring carnival's in town. You might find something there for Tasha."

Curling down, the bedspread reveals auburn hair and bloodshot eyes. "It's too late."

"I think there's still time."

"I'm not good at the games."

"You might win something for her. You might win something for me."

Lucas blushes.

"The longer you sit here, the less time you have to tell her goodbye."

He flops over and stares out the window where movers must be disassembling Tasha's room before they pack up and send her things and family to Cincinnati. Sidewalks, loose dogs, friendly cats, and chalk marks from the younger neighborhood kids fill the route Lucas walked from his house to hers, hers to his, through seasons of sharing the same classes in school until Mr. Sparks found his next opportunity in a place with an airport nowhere near Lucas, which meant, were he to fly there—if his mom had extra money, or if Tasha were to fly from there to see him—the airplane, he dragged his finger over his mom's laptop during his research, cruising at a speed far slower than spacecraft, would cross from central to eastern and back to central time while remaining in the same day.

Christine rubs his back. "I know it hurts. I had a friend who had to move. She was my one, really good friend. Come out when you're ready."

Drawings of alien vessels projecting a hologram meaning peace in their language and welcoming human fleets, flying their flags, shimmer under sunlight on Lucas's desk. He slides off the bed and hobbles back and forth between the kitchen and his doorway; the distance tires him. His mother clicking her laptop and the smell of coffee she brews on her weekends off from the distribution center float through the air. Lucas fidgets with a letter for Tasha he wrote last week after she told him she was leaving when the school year ended.

He props on the dining table. "What time is the carnival over?"

"This is their last weekend here."

"Oh." His left hip twitches.

"We should go." Christine double-taps her mouse. "They have an afternoon special. Ride one ride for free if you get tickets before four. And they have games." Pivoting her laptop, she shows Lucas the internet coupon.

"I guess we could."

"Be ready in thirty minutes?"

"Fifteen." He pulls a loose string near comets on his pajama top. "Do you think I could win something for her?"

"You'll know it when you see it."

His left foot dragging behind him, Lucas staggers to his bedroom and collection of far-away destinations and the means to reach them. In the carnival in his head—a crisp evening breezing over Tasha and him; the midway lights popping; aromas of fried food; creatures found in books or dreams rustling in the sideshows—he sits next to her and, as the sunset charges the sky, offers his jacket to her and holds her hand on the rides everyone else from school has talked about.

· · ·

On the first day of seventh grade, Lucas stepped into school without, for the first time in his life, immediate support. Principal Banks assured him and Christine that she, Nurse Richards, or Mr. LeDeux, Lucas's favorite counselor, would be down the hallway if Lucas needed them, but she encouraged him to navigate the spaces by himself while wishing him the best before greeting and sending along other students.

Most of the boys towered over Lucas—summer had broadened their shoulders and deeper tones cracked their voices; one boy pointed to a red speck where the razor nicked his chin. Lipstick and perfume adorned the girls Lucas had not seen since May, during which time he remained shaped like a question mark. Near the lockers, Mary Anne Reams, whose mother, before the front office promoted her, used to pick up Lucas's mom for the morning shift at the distribution center, did not say hi to him, as she had every day since the second grade; she smiled at him before turning away when her friends stopped her and handed out flyers for cheerleading and drama try-outs and chatted about books and movies they read or saw at swimming-pool parties or on vacations to lakes and cities. "Did you poop yourself?" asked one of the girls, glancing at Lucas's pants before staring at the single-arm crutch attached to his wrist. She closed her locker, her pigtails and flowery dress bobbing into the new semester with Mary Anne, who shied farther away, before Lucas could tell them that, on the school bus, he had sat on his power bar—the same food, he would have told them, delivered to the International Space Station.

Morning stretched between the halls as he stood alone among gossip, giggles, and after-school plans that did not include him. His backpack slumped to the back of his knees; the straps dragged near his untied shoe. His body shook; the curve of his spine and left hip dropped more; his eyes welled. He did not move until a hand took his. He did not know, had never seen, the girl guiding him through the crowds; her hold on him never let him look back. After she hugged him and nodded to her classroom across from his, Lucas asked her if he knew the vending machines outside the cafeteria. She shook her head no; the rainbow beads in her braids thumped against her long neck and matched the rubber bands in her mouth. Fishing a pen and scrap of paper from his pocket, Lucas highlighted them on a map he made for her, placing her at one end, him at the other, the sun and clouds over them and the school, and a straight line tethering them to the star marking where to meet.

They met there every day before lunch and ate at a table near the shrills of boys chasing girls, girls glancing at girls, boys wrestling boys, and the smells of food scraps dumped into trash cans. Tasha had moved to town when her father acquired a sales position that could ease the costs of hospital bills, doctor visits, and lawyers specializing in disability after automobile accidents. She told Lucas her father said any man who didn't move into the unknown and do whatever it took was no man. She left from the last place without saying goodbye to teachers and friends. She described her father as hungry more than angry, but sometimes it was hard to tell when money burned up as quickly as it had entered into his life. She squeezed a blueberry juice box while leaves dropped on the basketball court and wrote her home address for Lucas on a biology assignment she had earned ninety-six percent on. She was nervous about next week's cat dissection, because days after they had arrived in town her Jacko Jumping Bean disappeared, and said she expected, her lips blue, to move again.

Months later, sleet flaked the gray air, and before they had to return to class, after sharing PB&J sandwiches and candy, Lucas slid a stack of pictures tied under a ribbon and a card.

"Thank you." She opened the first one labeled Dr. Tasha Sparks MD and blushed at the stethoscope and colored-pencil green of her scrubs. Her nose wrinkled at the next image of her in surgery and the operating table. "Are all those hearts the patient's?"

"No." Lucas squinted; his small teeth exaggerated his gums as he smiled. "They're because of today."

"You must have used every red marker in town."

"You saved all these lives because you're the best in Jefferson County."

She opened the next batch—blueprints initialed L.D. alongside his address, phone number, and his mother's email.

"These are your copies. I'm sending the originals to NASA."

"What's that?" Tasha pointed to a circle on a ship's fuselage.

"Escape hatch." Lucas flipped three pages over and landed on a control panel's button. "They're not supposed to give up if things go wrong, but I want them to have it."

"They'll be in space, right? They'll need food, water. What if they float away?"

Lucas's shoulders collapsed.

"Becoming an astronaut is tough. You have to have be smart and have lots of strength."

"I know," he mumbled.

"But there's a job for anybody who wants it, if it has to be done," Tasha quickly continued. "Here."

He nudged the packet of flower seeds stickered with cartoon animals.

"They bloom at night," she said.

"Cool. Thank you."

"Happy Valentine's Day," they said to each other, hugging, ignoring their peers, who, throughout the first semester, had whispered about them and puckered lips in their direction, making kissing and moaning sounds, teasing them that their kids would be half-metal, half-this-and-that, walked by and ignored them—the black girl with braces on her teeth who had helped nurse her mother after the car wreck; and the white boy who designed vehicles for cutting deeper into the sky while his body pulled him closer to the ground.

. . .

After taking the receipt from the man wearing a top hat and glowing necklaces, Christine loops the tickets over her arm. Lucas snakes through the turnstiles and, his crutch pointing high in the spring air, across the midway's threshold. An increasing chance for a thundershower has not pushed away the crowds. Clowns wave. Witches on broomsticks coast by a spider towering on the façade of Dr. Mysterio's House of Horrors. Christine takes Lucas's free hand, but stepping into the pulses of screams and a calliope, he shakes her off. Kids from his school cross the main path in the distance; the afternoon sun brightens them when they laugh and share drinks or candy. Filling in behind them—families and strollers, college students, grey- and white-haired bikers wrapped in dark leather, and balloons loosened in bursts of wind.

"What would you like to do first?" she asks.

He looks left where booths blink and fewer people thread between them. More kids his age pass him on their way to The Tornado and its speakers blasting songs he's heard them obsess about; has listened to when he is on his mom's computer when he should be doing his homework; and after figuring out the keys and musical structures, created his versions on a keyboard Christine bought him after his father's funeral. He sent them to Tasha, who replied that if he ever ran for student council, he had found his soundtrack, which she loved. "Over there." He wobbles that way.

They walk past Test Your Grip and a man struggling with a brass ring drilled into a stone before the clock over him stops; children balancing on beams stretched between sea-green foam blocks tossed among pirate ships, mermaids, and sharks; and elderly couples shooting water pistols that propel miniature race horses and their marionette jockeys to the finish.

Christine stops at one of the snack shacks around the corners of the game booths as Lucas takes tickets to a pitcher's mound and stuffed animals. His father, before he left for Fallujah, showed Lucas fastballs, curves, sliders. Summer grilling and his parents toasting Lucas and his quick mastery of the knuckleball ended that evening, and as night deepened, the three of them counted blips in Orion's belt.

The attendant places a basket of baseballs at Lucas's feet lopsided on the foul line. His aim at the hole painted like a catcher's mitt worsens with each throw: a dribble into the fake grass; a drop behind his shoulder when he cocks his arm; a pitch so wild and slow it does not trigger the speed gun, which flashes a good-enough number for an extra pitch for a boy in the next cage who then wins his choice of prizes.

When one ball remains, the teenage attendant waits for a man, carrying a clipboard, to finish his rounds before she motions to Lucas that, checking over her shoulder, if he's quick, she'll let him inch past the foul line. He misses. The attendant lets him scoot more toward the middle. He misses again. Wiping mustard off her lips, Christine stands outside the netting. The attendant slides off her stool and points to a foot away from the target. Lucas lobs balls that thump off the edge of the hole and into the tray at the bottom. Nearby contestants murmur; a mother crosses her arms before marching over.

"That's enough," Christine says to the attendant, stepping inside the cage, one hand holding a box of cotton candy and soft pretzels, the other ushering Lucas. "Thank you."

On their way out, Lucas gazes at the boy who took the last stuffed giraffe.

After several rounds of video games in the arcade, plus the sideshows, artists, and musicians, few tickets remain, and clouds have thickened. Lucas and Christine head for the exit, retracing their steps through the midway where school kids, snorting and jumping around, press into a line winding around employees rinsing vomit off concrete. One of the boys sees Lucas and stiffens his arms and legs; his friends snicker, bug out their eyes, and gesture a mouthful of wires over their teeth.

Lucas's pace slows as though he asks his shadow to go on alone, but as UFO-shaped cars stop and the sides wing up at the stairs leading inside, he pivots. "I want to ride that."

Christine glimpses the seat belts as large as hoses and people trembling as they step off the ride. "I'm not riding that. We don't have enough tickets for you and me."

"OK." He holds out his palm.

His crutch banging metal and wood, he reaches the first step of the loading platform and trips on the toe guard. The operator's sunglasses flare as she checks her phone and smacks her gum. An attendant sits Lucas next to a middle-aged woman whose bliss spills across her children cheering from the grass; her wife, throwing kisses, reminds her their wills are up to date and jokes they'll name the next dog after her—she'll never be forgotten. The track hisses; the UFOs spring up, cock back; lights flash underneath. An alien voice counts down their ascent as they wait for the first loop before dropping into a valley and accelerating in a curve under the sky fading into dark gray.

But then warning bell rings. The ride powers down, having never moved; Lucas waits to be released. The crowds break up, clump, and dissipate again. Thunder rolls; rain falls. Managers mutter into headsets, motion to shut it all down, and show the way toward the main gate over which the alien ships would have sailed Lucas atop downtown, county farmlands, and Tasha's house, and would have placed him between soil and stars and above the horizon where he is least seen and where he could have been most known and faced it all from above and below.

. . .

Starting with pencil, Lucas sketches on a top sheet that, when enough tape connects the other sheets, will be a section of a galaxy he's learning about; a star on the outermost ring is fading. He's taken down concepts for engines and cockpits from the past year to make room for this latest project. He has kept up drawings of Tasha and him on a sailboat anchored to a volcano populated with tigers and eagles that are their friends; at the science fair where, as a team, they won honorable mention; and defeating dragons with names reminiscent of kids at school— Shane McStinkerbutt and NeverEverEvan, the latter at whom Tasha yelled in second period when she left for the day with her mother in pain after her father, in the sheen of morning ice and sleet, drove hours north for his interview in Cincinnati. Lucas opens a box of markers.

Christine knocks before opening his door. "I've tried calling over there, but no one's answering." She scrolls through her phone and notes the storm's passage and its warning's expiration. "I don't think she'd leave without saying goodbye." She strokes his hair. "Do you want to go over there?"

Lucas sighs at his drawing. The star starting to explode in graphite-and-pink blossoms across the paper's blank sky.

"It could be your last chance."

Lucas drops a marker—the supernova to finish collapsing another time. He handles his crutch, grabs his letter to Tasha, and starts for the garage, where, after the door lifts, remains of the day seep in; he disappears among cabinets and gardening supplies. Christine pulls out the minivan and idles alongside the soaked front yard and a narrow row of flowers, drooping but not broken, their colors waiting to open when the day crosses into tomorrow. Lucas holds a trowel and a grocery bag and digs up two of the flowers. Christine jogs into the garage and returns with a rubber band and paper towels; she offers a pen and a notepad. Lucas shakes his head and snaps the rubber band over his letter clasped between the smell of rain; the roots and blooms of Tasha's gift; and the night and lunar light returning in the sounds of thunder.

The minivan rattles to a halt, brakes squeaking, near Tasha's house. A large branch blocks the middle of the street. Before Christine backs up to circle it, Lucas opens the passenger door. His lithe frame stutters up the sidewalk leading to the driveway.

"Honey?" she yells as his silhouette balances walking and, on his crutch, the purple-and-white flowers and his letter. She pulls the minivan to the curb near the house and keeps the engine running.

Further up the street and deeper into evening Lucas staggers. He turns at the driveway, and the world and its border-light turns at the house where he saw her the most and where she still could be, if his timing is as right as first time he came over and the end-of-summer sun shone overhead.

The For Sale sign has been yanked out of the yard. Mr. Sparks's car is not in the driveway; the wheelchair ramp remains; the house is quiet and dim inside, curtains pulled. Lucas navigates smaller fallen branches until he stands at the front door.

"You're Tasha's friend," her father said that day.

"Yes, sir. Lucas Deetz."

Marvin smiled while Tasha stood behind him on the stairs and her younger brother snickered not at Lucas but at Tasha and Lucas waving to each other. "I've heard a lot about you. Come on in." He moved to the side of the door. "Watch your step." He offered to help Lucas before Lucas glided in by himself. "We got snacks in the kitchen. Tasha picked them out. I see you brought your computer."

"Yes, sir. It's my mom's. She's letting me borrow it for our homework. We have no idea what we're doing."

"But we got to figure it all out, Dad. Like now." Tasha quickly led Lucas to the living room.

"Good man," Marvin said.

Lucas knocks. Nothing. The clouds continue pushing east toward the river and the mountains; the moon rises between them and far-away stars alive and dying. He whispers her name like a plea carrying itself over houses and trees. Holding the letter snapped to its flowers, he rings the bell, settles his right heel, most of his weight on his crutch, his left hip shaking, the rest of him floating and unattached, waiting for the door to open in the light of evening reaching the ground.

Skeleton Key

Electrical problems on floors three through five flood my phone when I clock in after sunset. Unit 417 wonders if rats are building nests in our walls after the city demoed the hotels across the street. Poison, not traps, he suggests before closing his door because the snapping will wake his girlfriend's newborn.

Mrs. Hix leaves a voicemail while I remove a panel to inspect wires. I know you're down there. Please come up. I need help in here.

I've never been inside her place. All the work I've done for her has been exterior: paint, burned-out hallway lights, mud and leaves tracked in her hall, especially during the winter rains. I've never seen her enter or exit the complex. Any of her interior maintenance started and ended with my predecessor who handed the skeleton key to me on my first day. "All she's got left are the ravens on her windows."

Last summer I knocked to let her know I'd repair the HVAC before temps turned up. The heatwave hospitalized several residents. Not all of them returned. I trashed the stuff their families never came for. Of those who came back, most of them struggle walking to Social Security. "If it gets too hot, I'll use my broomstick to get out," Mrs. Hix told me through her cracked door. Her voice warbled then but not as much as in her second voicemail in less than ten minutes. Hurry. Please. She wheezes like my wife's tío Jimmy did near his end.

I double-check the panel screws and load my tool cart. The elevator moans, screeches, stalls out. I pump the up button and pry open the doors. Silence relieves me after I ask if anyone is on there.

While my phone dings, I kill the elevator's power and tape OUT OF ORDER. Fire sprinklers domino down the hall. Units creak open. Residents bulge their eyes. Some shuffle for the exits. A woman in an end unit thumbs at the stairwell. Three teen girls hide their lighter when I find them. I apologize to everyone for the false alarm, the scare, the inconvenience. They tell me to tell the property manager to kiss their butts. I call off the fire department, and the sunset covers us with oranges and yellows spun from the ocean. The teen girls flip me the finger after I yell at them. In another message, Mrs. Hix chants.

I lock my cart in place, cinch my tool belt, climb the stairs. The door to the sixth floor jams. My boots scuff the wall as I brace myself. The knob loosens, but my next yank snaps it off, and I tumble down the flight. My voicemail buzzes as I stare from my back into the skylight and the day's last hour scattered across bricks and beams. My head aches. My tongue and throat swell, ears ring, legs freeze. Blood warms my wrist and shin and seeps into my pants. The screwdrivers and hammer missed my ribs. My fall, not the night, twinkles across my eyes. Silhouettes of palm trees flap but, unlike wings, don't go anywhere.

"Anything else I can help you with?" I asked Mrs. Hix another time through her door.

"The spikes in rent. They smother us."

"I know. I'm sorry, but that's out of my hands."

"Then I'll give you more. I need a lock of your hair."

"Ma'am?"

"I can summon you through other dimensions."

"My wife won't be too thrilled if you mess that up."

"I have a grimoire to protect you. Besides, the dead give more than the living ever can."

The door muffled her shuffling away.

The handrails I tightened last fall help me off the ground and all the way to the roof where air drifting in from the coast chills me and graffiti spots the low walls. Arrows connect hearts. Hands embrace hands. Names and dates scribbled in, struck out. RECYCLE RENEW REUSE. NOT THE FINISH BUT THE CHASE. A NEW COMMUNITY. A sequence spray-paints storms into rainbows.

Past the wood-rot, concrete chunks, spiderwebs, roaches, and crows on power lines, the far-off observatory sits in the hills like an eyeball. Monique and I stopped on a whim, driving back from our son's birthday at my parents' house. We lifted Ben to the telescope until he saw the starlight that would reach us but only after they're long gone.

I climb down the other roof-access ladder and turn the corner for Mrs. Hix's floor.

"Mrs. Hix?"

No answer from inside when I knock.

"Mrs. Hix!"

Nothing.

I fumble for my skeleton key.

Neighbors step out, whisper, huddle. The smells of spices from their kitchens spill into the hall where noises rise and fall. My head spins. My phone squawks. The sun sets lower into the horizon turning dark blue under the rising moon.

The door unlocks. Black birds scatter from the windows. A breeze chimes silver stars dangling between curtains. Candles flicker over Mrs. Hix's outstretched body. Shadows unfold behind me, and those shadows shadow more shadows.

I call 9-1-1 and step across the threshold.

An overturned stool. Rings of water from fallen plants. Trinkets, playing cards with illustrations, photos of maybe her husband, kids, grandkids. Greeting cards and letters stacked alongside a recliner and near the collapsed bookshelf I would've moved for her. A book lies open to black-and-white spirals splitting two women down the middle. The young woman lifts wheat from morning to noon and passes it to the old woman who scatters it after it breaks into seeds.

The ambulance wails down the street. I see in my head, at home, Monique reading to Ben until he falls asleep under his drawings of constellations. But here, more doors open and close, and more rooms empty. Lips murmur prayers. Footfalls above and below surround us. The echoes of it all caught between silence coming and going and a baby crying.

Clean Slate

Coffee cup in hand, a judge crosses the lane dividing booths. Shipping boxes and containers—cardboard, plastic, and climate-controlled; fliers, signs, and banners; and kegs, single bottles, and six packs—multiply the maze of vendors and exhibitors streaming inside the exposition center and near the loading docks where Gerald emerges with a table he sets on a hand-truck and wheels to a middle booth. The judge throws his hips out of the way, dodging a collision, but the table's edge taps the coffee cup.

"Sorry about that," Gerald says. The raven, singing NEVERMORE! and perched upon a skull inked along his forearm, snatches a towel off the hand-truck.

"No harm, no foul. It's a busy morning."

Gerald glimpses the judge's lanyard. "And now I'm really sorry. Don't chop off any zeroes from the prize."

The judge points to WATERMELON MTS. BREWERY on the booth. "Where are you from?"

"Albuquerque."

"Congrats on getting in. It gets tougher and tougher. Well, thank you for…"

Gearld rears up. "Have we got a stout for you. Best one here."

The judge clutches his clipboard closer to his gut.

"We got high marks for it at Four Corners Brew Fest."

"That's a good one. Congrats. I need to…"

"We lost to some IPA infused with weed from Boulder hippies. They were giving the judges weed on the side. Probably. But an IPA? Everybody from the West coast to the Rockies brews IPAs. That's lacy fairy wings and rainbow bubbles. But a stout…that's black magic. Like a deal with the Dark Lord."

The judge smiles politely.

"You don't need to try anybody else." Gerald looks toward his booth's loading dock where silhouettes grab items from an SUV. "If you give me a sec, I can get you a preview."

The judge waves to men and women wearing lanyards. "Good luck today. I'll see you this afternoon."

"You should start with ours first." Gerald pops out the table legs. "It stands on its own." His black-painted thumbnail jabs at the booth as the judge's bald head moves down the other half of the expo until it disappears among mohawks, crewcuts, ponytails, ball caps, and more bald heads.

A pony keg clanks behind Gerald who winks at his brother twisting the dolly from underneath.

"You putting a spell on them up already?"

"Just chatting with the locals."

Mark laughs. "They can turn on us."

"But if you feed them right, they'll never bite you. Speaking of…Ang, we got any of those breakfast sandwiches left?"

Angie helps a young boy step down from the SUV before slinging a newborn. "Babe, did you eat the last one?"

"Nope," Mark says. He unpacks a display and reaches for an extension cord in a bin by his work boots. "Carl, did you have it?"

The young boy shakes his head no and spreads out his drawing pads and colored pencils on a table Angie sets up for him in the booth's corner. He pulls from his backpack a dragon-stenciled headband, its tail wrapped around the red fabric, slides it over his mop of hair, and sighs over his sketch of a cathedral and its spires stretching toward the sun and moon tethered by a chain of flowers.

"I'll go look. If…I…have enough…energy." Gerald feigns fainting from hunger. He pats his jeans' pockets. "Besides, I left my phone in the car." He stops near Carl. "That's looking good."

"I wish I had it done for today. It could be on a bottle like yours."

"Next time."

"Uncle Ger?"

"Yeah, bud?"

"What could we call it?"

He scratches his beard. "Flower Towers Saison. Better finish it. We'll need it." He winks and heads for the loading dock.

Angie and Mark top off the table display with its watermelon crowning beer bottles arranged into mountain peaks. Carl giggles but becomes serious when he faces his artwork and arranges his colored pencils. Mark finds the outlet and slides a switch to his wife who flicks it on. They kiss each other before kissing the newborn asleep in the sling. The watermelon and mountain-top beer bottles glow pink.

Inside the SUV, Gerald uncovers his phone from beneath a stained and wrinkled copy of the festival's schedule highlighting the Tasting Grand Prize and its amount; in the margins—Mark's calculations for new equipment, additions to the brewery, more marketing; on the reverse side—Gerald's scribbles and ideas for labels and brands. But the screen flashing NEW VOICEMAIL – SIMONE sinks Gerald into the backseat and the inked tree spreading its bare branches from his sternum up and across his collarbone, its roots twisting out her name. His knee and jaw twitching, he listens to Simone from a place she calls him into, whenever they talk, where he waits among the past's dazzling parts that the present has not yet sealed.

He shuffles back to the booth where Mark and Angie's laughter rises into snorts as she flexes her hips, shimmies her hair down her back, and exaggerates pouting lips.

"Ang says she'd be willing to show a lil' something for the judges, if we have to sweeten our chances. This is our year. She's prayed about it more than ever."

Gerald chuckles and rubs his phone.

"The judges can sneak a peek," Angie says. "But I'll make it look like an accident."

Crowds increase after the main doors open. The baby tugs Angie.

"The judges might be seeing more than that." Angie slides Ramona under her shirt. "More importantly, when are we going to sabotage our competition?" A grin slices her face.

"Dad always says Ang is the daughter he'd been waiting for."

Gerald ignores his brother's long-running joke.

"Some heavy hitters here." Mark wipes his palms. "I hope they meet and greet…find us. Maybe they're scouting up-and-comers." He digs out tasting-notes sheets. "It can be like a pebble starting a rock slide."

"No buy-outs." Angie pulls out Ramona. "Small batches. Small circle of influence. Ours. All ours."

"Carl, Mommy and Daddy are talking business. You doing OK?"

The young boy doodles.

Mark turns to Gerald who hides his phone in his hoodie. "What's up?"

"Simone left a message."

"Aunt Simone!" Carl shouts. "Is she coming? She missed my birthday."

Gerald smiles at his nephew before turning to Mark, but when he reaches Angie, he turns away. "She wants to talk this weekend."

"Always perfect timing from her. I bet she knows the prize amount. Gee, I wonder what she'd do with it."

"Ang," Mark intervenes.

She blinks at Gerald. "Isn't that what she wants?"

"Maybe." His jaw cocks while he shrugs. "Maybe not."

. . .

The PA system buzzes. *Tom and Hector from Coyote 95.1 Classic Rock will be on the main stage until two this afternoon to meet fans, sign autographs, and play trivia with some pints before they join our judges for the Tasting Grand Prize at three. Come on by, say hi, make a good guess, and you might end up on the air with a coupon to Gondola Pizza and any of their Phoenix locations.*

"Free Bird!" a man in shorts yells through a megaphone he fashioned from a cup.

Some in the crowd around him jeer, play invisible guitars, and raise finger-horns.

Gerald covers his ear, turns his back toward the booth's corner, but when Angie cruises by, holding a basket of hops and a diagram of beer production, and Simone's voicemail answers, he hangs up.

And don't forget to cast your votes for the People's Choice Award while you're making your way around.

Free Bird's questions about a beer Mark pours rise in volume; people bubble around him and motion to friends and neighbors.

Mark casts a plea toward Gerald and Angie before fumbling answers and staggering back to the man's sunburned face.

"You know that's not his thing." She hands Gerald the basket, the diagram, and media he designed. "Simone's not going anywhere." She puffs her hair and sets a rose behind an ear. "She needs to wait for us. Go be his big brother. Please."

Gerald sighs before shaking the flyers. "Folks, this man is the brewmaster!" His skinny arm cloaks Mark wiping sweat. "He made everything you're tasting."

"Good stuff," Free Bird says.

"Not just good, my friend. This is the best of good ol' American microbreweries. One-hundred-percent grit and love from an Anglo-Mexican family. Blue eyes and green chiles." Gerald motions to Mark, Angie, and the kids. "You look like you're a golfer."

Free Bird tips his visor. "This morning before here."

"But the rest of you day is about to start…for the better."

The man and crowd tighten as Gerald pops open a tall bottle —skulls, bones, and stones stamped on the glass and as black as a burn.

"This is our latest. My brother worked it until he got it right." Gerald lines up cups and pours streams of night. "We offer you Catacombs Extra-Dark Stout."

"This is way better than that." Free Bird nods at the cup Mark filled with a lager. "No offense."

"None taken," Mark replies, his color returning.

"But the lager pairs well with fish," Gerald quickly says. "I bet you fish too."

"I do."

"You should pick up our lager. We had a guy last week tell us it brought out the rosemary in his salmon."

"Nope. Just grill and butter for me."

Angie slides forward. "How does ten percent off sound?"

Free Bird's head cocks. "Maybe. The stout is better."

"Anything special in the recipe?" A woman examines a bottle for sale.

"Something to do with Paris," Gerald answers.

"You put dead people in here?" snickers one of the trio of college-aged men.

"I promise my wife is not in there." Gerald crosses an X over his black hoodie.

The crowd laughs.

"Be sure to vote for us and make note of who we are and what you had. Even our lager," Angie says, turning from the crowd to Gerald. "We have some goodies." She passes out branded coasters and pushes play on the laptop she set on the table. "And we have a little video about us."

"Our Fiesta Pilsner is named after our COO. Better yet…buy some here or when you're in Albuquerque." Gerald motions to a pony keg and its image of a long-legged señora curling her crimson dress across snow-capped mountains tinted pink on the crest.

Angie curtsies; blows kisses.

"And our stout is up for the Tasting Grand Prize."

As more people stop by, sample the beers, and chat with Mark and Angie, Gerald slips away, saying he needs to use the restroom and refill his coffee. He walks toward concessions, and when the booths fade, he sits at a table closest to the back and hidden by grill smoke, signs and menus, and cash registers and condiments. He reaches for his phone. MISSED CALL – SIMONE. Her voicemail answers—first in English; second in French.

<Hey do you mind coming back to get Carl?> Mark's texts light up Gerald's screen. <He wants to get a snack with you.>

When Gerald returns, the video loops to the start. *A few years ago, we did something crazy. We started a microbrewery with our savings and zero experience.*

"Uncle Ger!"

"Yeah, buddy. What shall we get?"

"Nothing too sugary." Angie grabs the diaper bag.

I combined my love of home-brewing and my HVAC skills.

"Kettle corn? Funnel cake? Caramel apple?" Gerald asks.

"All of that?" Carl's eyes bug out as he sets aside his drawings.

I took my know-how of accounting and love of everything having to do with family.

"One, Carlos." Heading to the SUV, Angie throws a look at Gerald who chuckles.

"Hey man, thanks for earlier. You worked your magic again."

Gerald shows Mark nothing up his hoodie's sleeves save for the gray-purple bands inked over his wrists.

And I moved back to America from France and applied my design background to help my younger brother and his wife.

Gerald takes Carl's hand as they stand in line. His phone vibrates, and as he's ready to answer, Carl changes his mind, but Gerald doesn't see root-beer float listed on the menu.

"She has one." Carl points to a girl walking through sunlit doors.

"You got it." Before the doors close, Gerald spots a food truck painted with ice-cream cones, sundaes, and milkshakes flanked by cacti. Parked on the pavement, its awning boxes out a shade over sand. "Let me hear something before we go." He pats a seat, where Carl flops onto, and plugs his ear, but noise and static cut the beginning and middle of Simone's message. He checks when she called while handing his credit card to the server. *Until I go to bed…call me if you can* reaches Gerald and pulls him into brighter light.

"It's hot." Carl drags his headband down and up, wiping sweat and foam. "Can I have two?"

"You can some of mine." Gerald offers a bite of his ice-cream sandwich. "But don't tell your mom. And you have to draw something for me. You have to finish it before we leave."

Carl taps his chin; his face mushes. "Hmm…OK."

After they return to the booth, Angie asks, "Did you sneak something on the side for him?"

"Me? No way."

"He'll end up telling me anyway after I ask what he got. He can't keep a secret."

Gerald looks around: Mark chews a sandwich, chats with a brewmaster, and rocks Ramona; the lager they brought is half gone, and the stout disappeared; and Angie opens another round of pilsners and chats with an owner about wanting the company to grow but on their terms—not influenced by outside money or anything "too corporate." Gerald grumbles, "The show's slipping. We got to get our star back on stage."

Make it happen Angie's face says.

He rolls out another pallet of Catacombs from the SUV but stops when the heat brings an image of Simone extending her hand to Gerald in renewing their vows during the nights that excited them; he turns for Simone, but she disappears into the city and the desert under the city and its network of land that time cycled through and cleared. Air conditioning kicks on above Gerald and rattles the loading dock. The sun silhouettes figures inside the exposition center, but Gerald knows the shapes of

Mark stretching his back, Ramona tight against his chest, promoting what they have and plan for in the future, and talking up the beer and Gerald's marketing but talking down sales; Angie looping her arm in Mark's and talking up their donations to veteran organizations, shelters, and their church; and Carl, hidden behind the booth, copying Gerald's labels where they lay scattered, alongside blueprints and loan applications, in Mark and Angie's kitchen. People multiply around the booth. And Mark and Angie searching for Gerald summon him as much as Simone and a future neither he nor Simone have settled on and could build from.

"There he is," Mark says to Gerald appearing from the rear of the booth.

Looking up from swiping a credit card, Angie smiles.

"Last call before the Grand Prize!" Gerald yells. "Try a winner before it's the winner!" He pops open two fresh bottles as distant lights grow and voices call him.

*   *   *

After they deliver a bottle of Catacombs to the judges' assistants and confirm their entry form, they wedge in among contestants and fans who hollow around Mark when he unfolds a chair for Angie and Ramona. The emcee introduces the judges, including the radio DJs and, selected from the crowd, a woman representing the People's Choice Award.

"You did give them the one we set aside, right?" Mark asks. "By the diaper bag."

"Oh shit."

Mark pales and rubs his whiskers.

"It was the right one." Gerald wraps his arm around his brother, and his kiss reddens Mark's cheek. "I cut my finger to write BARRIÈRE D'ENFER on a piece of paper I taped to the cap."

"What's that mean?"

"Gates of Hell."

"Please tell me you told Carl this. Maybe drew a little pentagram on his backpack. Or showed him how to do it."

A woman turns around, shushing and glaring.

As the first round opens—wheat ales—Gerald's phone murmurs in his hoodie.

<Hi. It would be nice to talk today. Hope the festival is bringing you bliss. Maybe you're out celebrating :) >

Gerald gnaws his lip while he covers his phone.

Excellent citrus notes rings the microphone on the main stage. *I would serve this, especially after a run on the slopes, and pair sharp cheddar and honey crackers with it. Nice job.* Mark focuses on the judges and crowd. Angie gives a bag of carrot sticks to Carl who, drawing pad across his knees, sits next to her.

Gerald texts <We're at the contest now.>

<Oh you're around. Hi. I bet you're winning!>

<We're not up yet. Just started.>

<Which one is yours?>

<The stout I told you about.> He pauses. <Inspired by one of our favorite spots in the city.>

<More than that! The night never stopped wherever we were.>

<No it never did.> He presses the phone into his waist when Mark claps and the microphone squawks *Let's move on to brown ales. First up…Maple Brown from Opelika Hops.* <So what's going on?>

<I don't want to text now you're around. Talk in person.>

Gerald scans the area—few people and vendors not attending the contest. "I gotta hit the head."

"OK," Mark replies, half-looking at Gerald. "Hurry back."

Carl turns around, offers a drawing to his uncle who has vanished, and taps Angie's elbow as Gerald excuses himself through the crowd.

Inside a shadow far away from the main stage, Gerald speaks into his phone, disagreeing but then agreeing with Simone, nodding yes again and again as though they stand in the dark on the verge of retreating as light seeps in and forms a stairwell up and out for them. After hanging up, he thanks anything above that listened to him.

"Hey." Angie approaches. "Carl was looking for you." She bobs as Ramona coos.

"I had to use the bathroom."

She glances at his phone before he hides it in his hoodie. "You talking to Simone?"

"Yeah."

"And?"

Gerald waits until a couple drifts into the crowd and the microphone introduces another entry. "It's promising. Sounds like. It'll be good."

Angie's stare narrows. "She said as much?"

"She didn't say anything about divorce or counseling."

"You're starting over with it? With her?"

Gerald shrugs. "We didn't bring that up yet."

"Is she coming here? Or are you going there?"

"That's down the road."

The crowd's grumbles revolve into cheers.

"Don't go back to her. You'll be back under debt again from chasing all those highs the two of you couldn't keep up with."

"That's not me anymore."

"Exactly. You can pull back now, but she won't. She hasn't changed, Gerald."

"You don't know that. And neither do I. This could end up being a fresh start."

Angie frowns. "If you leave, you'll end up worse off. And, I'm not gonna lie, for us too. We have something here. What we've done. This has kept you focused. You got better footing."

Up next will our last beers of the day.

The crowd tightens.

"We did this with you, and you did this with us."

The stouts!

After Angie leaves for the main stage, Gerald pulls out his phone. <Gotta go. We'll talk soon. I love you.> His finger hovers over Send. Mark turns from the crowd and lifts Carl onto his shoulders. The boy's feet drums his dad's chest when Angie arrives. As Carl points to Gerald and they wave him back in, he quickens his pace and keeps his message in place.

· · ·

They pack most of their booth but keep out unsold bottles and smaller merchandise for stragglers ambling from the crowd into the summer glowing as evening comes on. A judges' assistant informs them to return to the main stage in ten minutes and checks off her clipboard before walking to a vendor two rows over.

"She's speaking to them longer," Mark mutters, fluxing between wiping tables and spying. His thick brow and shoulders slump. "Now she's laughing with them."

"Maybe they know each other." Gerald squints that way. "They have the Arizona flag for their brand. They could've done something better with that label. I could've."

"They don't have you," Angie says.

"No, they do not."

"Now they're waving goodbye to each other, and she's pointing to another area of the stage." Mark nearly trips, stretching on his toes. "I think it's the front. Damn. Yeah. She didn't point us there."

"So, you're saying Ang didn't show enough T&A?"

She lounges on the chair like a pin-up girl and blows kisses. "We did good today. More people know about us. We had more sales than last year." She nods at the laptop's spreadsheet. "And we have fewer boxes of everything to take back." She turns to Gerald. "All for you to get on social media about."

He blushes. "I've been meaning to update in real time."

"We're still here." She half-smiles and returns to cleaning.

"Did you see that judge's response with that one stout from Dallas?" Mark flips a table on its side. "He was in another orbit."

"He's one of five."

"But he was the most vocal. The rest took cues from him."

"Could be for show."

"I should have cut back on the coffee on that batch. Or we could have set aside that other batch for them and sold the others."

"That one judge liked it." Gerald rolls a banner. "And this is one contest out of how many? There are more."

Angie quickly snaps his way.

"There's that big one in Kansas City," Mark says. "You have to prove a certain amount of sales and market reach."

"That's not our neck of the woods," Angie replies as the laptop powers down.

"Not yet." Mark overlooks the bare booth. "The prize money gets us there."

"What about our loans?"

Mark says to Angie, "It's in the fall so I can come up with a pumpkin-something. Who doesn't love Halloween? Right, Carl?"

"It's my favorite besides the Tooth Fairy, but I have to lose teeth for that." His tongue pokes out as he scribbles.

Gerald winks at his nephew. "Everyday should be Halloween."

The PA clicks on. *While our judges finish deliberating, now's a good time to plan for next year. Stop by our promotions table by the main stage and sign up for news, updates, and more. In the meantime, sit tight with the day's last calls from our fantastic vendors as we await division winners and the winner of our Tasting Grand Prize.*

"Maybe a cider," Mark says. "Haven't done a cider yet. Might be good to stretch ourselves that way. What do you think?" He turns to Gerald. "I know we talked about some more marketing. And knocking down our loans." He turns to Angie who agrees while picking up Ramona.

"Well…" Gerald glances at the text sitting on his phone. "I wanted to talk to you about that. If we win, I want us to split it. And I'd like to have the cash."

Mark leans in. "You need help again?"

"No, he doesn't."

Gerald glances at Angie glaring at him. "I want to use it for travel. I'd like to get Simone here with it. Or maybe I go there."

Carl gathers up his art supplies. "Do I have time to use the bathroom? I'm also hungry."

"Yes, you do, sweetie." Angie takes him while slinging Ramona.

"Man, I disagree with that. Big time."

"I knew you would."

"Angie would feel the same way."

"You're two for two."

"And if we win, she will not be down with Simone getting our money after what we did to get here."

OK, folks, it's time. Our judges are ready to announce our winners!

"Do you want to cash out entirely? Leave this?"

Gerald scratches the back of his head where the script ÉTERNITÉ sits. "We're making it up as we go."

"What about when all the partying with her ends? Like before?"

Gerald looks at and away from his brother.

"Your honeymoon phase crashed down to Earth pretty quick."

Let's start with the People's Choice Award.

The crowd claps, smaller than when the judging started. The brothers fall silent. Angie, standing outside restrooms, turns their way, her arms crossed.

"Not us," Mark says, grimacing as silhouettes appear onstage and accept their trophy and money.

"We should head over there."

"Have you said anything to Carl about this?"

"No."

They meet up with Angie who readies a water bottle, half a banana, a spoon, and a tub of peanut butter.

OK, let's move on to the lagers.

Carl emerges from the restroom and flicks his fingers. Concessions shutter for the day. People stumble out of the exposition center; hard light takes them in. Carl says something to Angie who agrees after Mark answers, "Go now." After they return, Carl's backpack swings from his mother's hand, and Carl and Angie reach Mark and Gerald among the crowd by the main stage. The boy fidgets with a piece of paper.

Next up…brown ales.

Slipping behind his mother and father, Carl tugs Gerald. "I have something for you."

"Hey, hold on, Carl," Angie says, leaning down. Ramona fusses until Angie finds the pacifier. "We're almost done."

"What does he need now?" Mark asks, massaging his neck, his focus rolling between the stage and his son.

Congratulations. And next…the IPAs.

"This is for you," Carl murmurs.

"Thank you," Gerald whispers, smiling.

And now we're gonna change things here at the end because the winner of our stouts division is also the winner of our Tasting Grand Prize.

Gerald opens the drawing: space beneath a vault, its flanks shrinking as mountains and a road sink into the horizon cutting behind the roof and a sun flooding the floor and five figures— three adults; two children—holding cups and wearing medals; its walls wiped clear as though the rocks eroded away and anything unattached floats through the frames; its ribs rolling into a point overhead and, like wires carrying sounds, chanting to Gerald *Something new tops something old that had nowhere else to go.* The crowd tightens around Gerald as the PA speakers relay the result above, under, around but not yet through him. The crowd's whooping echoes through metal and into heat. Angie palms her mouth and slumps into Ramona and Mark whose hands drop from his neck as he exhales. Carl's smile cuts through the commotion. The result reaches Gerald and straightens him. He checks his phone and hits backspace on the message until the cursor stands alone in the open.

Like Land Does

The pump gets going, and I call Agee's from inside my car. Music from the Jeep parked next to me is too much to talk over. Nor do my ears like it. Agee's says I am more than welcome to add something small to Mother before they proceed—and they will wait for me. "Call us when you can. Let us know where you're close. We're happy to stay open for you until you get here." They've been so patient, like answers arriving from afar.

I step out when my tank clicks full. The Jeep with college students tips when the boys return from the store and hand beer to the girls in the back. One of them offers a can to me. He says it pairs well with Pop Tarts, which he pulls from a plastic bag, for a day on the lake. I laugh and tell him no thanks and to watch out for that exit—OHP likes to post there. He turns his ball cap backward and toasts me before checking bungees on jet skis. The music fades as the Jeep's doors close. Its red paint is blotched like insect spots.

A few semis cruise through the parking lot or rumble alive. Landscapers take a break from mowing. A delivery-truck driver jabbers with them before loading a dolly. No one honks at me to have my pump or pulls into empty stalls. My legs are already numb from the first hour of sitting—a few more left. Last week I told Mother I couldn't get there fast enough. "And then I'll be back down here again to get you." Us old gals can grab dinner tonight in spirit and then, when she's with me for good, whenever we want. I told Agee's I'd rather they not ship her to me.

Sixty miles from Paris, I pull over because I miss a voicemail. Traffic spurts by. The message clicks in and out with "Gwen from Ladybug" before dropping dead. Rain and wind pick up in the distance. Most of the morning darkens down near the border and toll bridge.

Half of me expects Ladybug to be the same as it's been but with more rust and holes in the tin roof, more rotted wood, most of the shutters closed up real tight for the summer storms, and all the walls and floors swollen thick like ticks. A couple from Natchitoches bought the store after Mr. Carl died. Mother and I went there whenever I was in town. They updated the front register with a computer, added online sales, and with a spreadsheet, can hunt down the smallest antique on the shelves or in any of those stuffed rooms. Mr. Carl had that precision. I had that same kind of precision until I turned sixty. Mother did too.

But the new owners haven't kept up with one of Mr. Carl's traditions. When he came back with the item you asked him about, he'd ring you up and slip into your bag the receipt and a small ladybug pin a little bigger than the real thing but as bright green and pink as the store's front door and trim. No space for advertising anywhere on that pin—not an insignia or abbreviation. But no matter where we were, Mother always stopped someone wearing one. "Did you get that from Ladybug in Shreveport?" The answer was always yes. Hers disappeared in the move to assisted living.

When I got hold of Gwen the other day, I asked if they had any pins left and said I'd pay any price for one. "I'll be in town this Saturday to get it." She thought her husband might know and would check with him and get back to me. She said she remembered me when Mother and I visited the store, but I'm not so sure. Mother's health limited our trips around the same time Mr. Carl's health declined.

I cross the Red River at the WELCOME TO TEXAS sign. Mother should have the ladybug pin on her before she's cremated.

• • •

"Anything else I can get you?"

I tap my mug. "A top-off, please. And do you have a to-go cup?"

"Sure thing."

The waitress grabs a water pitcher and a coffee pot but heads to a table down from my booth, which squeaks the deeper I rub my sore back and hips into it. Humidity has swollen my limbs behind the wheel, and my orthopedic shoes can't do their job while I'm driving.

Gwen answers when I call Ladybug but quickly says, "Hang tight. I got a customer."

The lunch crowd thins out, but the table my waitress helps remains the loudest. The kids run in circles, and every family member from end to end and in between plays with them as they gallop pass. Crumbs fall all over the floor. A condiments-bottle fight nearly breaks out. The men cross their arms, watch TVs in the corners, and entice the kids. The women flutter napkins, like they're fainting, while praising their apple, chocolate-coconut, and pecan pies. I adjust my hearing aid. Clinks and chatter chime inside me like someone slapping sheet metal.

The line between Gwen and me drops and becomes busy when I try again and again.

The waitress fills my mug and to-go cup and slides the check toward me. "Take your time."

"Thanks for calling Ladybug. We're unable to come to the phone…"

Outside, clouds puff up like the padded backs of booths emptying around me. The clock ticks near one-thirty. A cook and two men leaning on the counter can't wait for the Longhorns to open their season.

"Let me pay. My treat. I'm so proud of you," Mother said at a table in another restaurant. Red-and-white-checkered paper napkins. Reprints of newspapers, signs advertising household goods, and farm and kitchen tools fastened to the walls. She told the owner the mason jars we drank from could get a good price, were he to sell them. "But nothing wrong in keeping them for yourself," she added. Her grandmothers reused similar jars after they cleaned out jellies to spread on biscuits no bigger than the scraps of land her family spared from the Great Depression and the Dust Bowl.

Gray winter rain mushed against the windows that day. Before we ate, Mother toasted me. Her voice warbled, but she kept composed. My GED sat in its envelope on her kitchen counter. I had it mailed there after I started over. Earning it— between working any hourly wage available to me and taking care of her—left little in me. I smiled, not because of my effort but because I had finished. The website that helped me study said NEVER TOO LATE.

Mother rummaged through her purse and started for my car to search there. I stopped her as she tripped on her walker. On the drive to and from Ladybug that day she wondered if her brother had misplaced her money. My credit card with the lowest balance paid for our meals. I didn't tell her Uncle Dennis died ten years ago, after Aunt Ruth.

We spent hours cruising the aisles on that trip to Ladybug.

"Stay all day," Mr. Carl said.

"We sure can get lost here," Mother said.

"I'll tie a string to you so you can find your way back." His smile was as bright as his bowtie's stripes.

We found a baseball bat Mother thought maybe Uncle Dennis played with when he was young. Her fingers danced along the barrel and crossed a player's name etched near the end. I told her, no, that's not Dennis's because of the year listed under the name. She smelled the bat and agreed but only because her father carved Dennis's bat from a tree struck dead by lightning. He used the rest of the wood to prop her bedding off the dirt floor. She couldn't forget that smell as she lay under a roof patched thin enough that a bucket, used during the day for milk from surviving cows, collected prayed-for rain.

"Hi, Helen, I'm sorry about earlier," Gwen says while I pay my tab at the counter. "I have some good news. My husband knows what you're talking about. He saw the pins the other day in storage. After he's done loading an order, he'll head over there for you. I told him to grab as many as he can. The whole box even."

"Oh, that is wonderful. Thank you…thank you."

My back pain eases. I barely notice my hearing aid. My foot thumps the gas pedal. The sky is as blue as the veins in my hands —like Mother's.

. . .

Before the highway curves south, traffic gridlocks into a parking lot. None of this construction showed up on the GPS, which spins finding an alternate route before I kill it. Large trucks carry slabs of new road across rubbles of the old. All the honking behind and ahead of me and all the front fenders creeping up on the rear cannot budge any of us. I tap my to-go coffee, and before my phone had no bars, Agee's asked me if I wanted Mother's hands in a certain position for cremation— resting at her side, crossing her lap, or praying over her heart. "At her side," I told them. "Like she's asleep on her back." I almost said, "Like she fell asleep by a fire." I considered the prayer position. She only missed church when she couldn't go. The nursing home's chaplain ended up visiting her room. I only went to church to take her when I was in town. I sang hymns and followed along with sermons but nothing more than that.

A woman alongside me refuses to let in the station wagon and its moving boxes, dogs, kids, and the driver's middle finger. The opposite lanes heading north and west slow down but do not stop. Two cranes rise behind the woods lining the shoulders. If only they could bust open a passage for me, lift me out of here, guide me over the creeks and trees, and set me down where I need to be before sunset, like promises in the Bible.

We tighten down to one lane after a while and stand still again. My bladder and leg pains spread. I put my car in park, slide out, cross the ditch, and shuffle for the woods. Someone yells, "Get back in your car!" which bounces in my ears until trunks, leaves, and shadows cover me. I brace myself against bark I hope isn't poison oak, drop my pants, and relieve myself.

Late March one year I took time off from work, and Mother and I made it to New Orleans. Her walker fit in the minivan I had. We strolled, paused, backed up, stepped aside, started again, paused again, especially at the street musicians. Mother owned one record that perked up Mr. Carl when we stopped on our way. A 1950s first printing of a jazz pianist.

"How's the condition?" he asked her.

"Good scratches. The kind you know where you were."

"Where is it?"

"Wrapped in cloth in my sewing room."

"How did you get it?"

"I bought it with my first-ever check when I worked a Sears & Roebuck counter. It was money I didn't have to send back home."

"How much would you want for it?"

"That's got no price."

Tourists in New Orleans whizzed past us, and Easter could not quickly redeem whatever those crowds said, thought, kissed, and drank. We ate at most of the restaurants on our list but had to scale back. Mother ate like a rabbit. Rich food tangled up her stomach. I stopped in a pharmacy for antacid tablets, but her dentures sent me back for a liquid version.

Her back slumped, her eyelids drifted, her complaints and confusion increased, but she still wanted to walk the tour of the Quarter. We were the last group. More than halfway through the tour, near a cemetery, Mother had to use the bathroom, but none was around, and our starting and return point was far away. Stores were nowhere near us. I suggested adult diapers for the future, which set her off. The group wandered tombs and left us alone. On the other side of the cemetery, alongside a patch-job brick wall, hedges rose to our hips as dusk set in.

"Just go," I said, standing in front of her, handing napkins from my purse.

The guide pointed out, because of the city below sea level, all the tombs rest above ground. The bodies break down in heat, but it goes so slow.

"No."

"Please, Mom."

"No."

"No one will know."

"There're windows over there."

"Then wet yourself if you want to."

"I'm not a baby."

"You're so goddamned bullheaded. Piss or hold it in."

A few people in the group stared at me after I yelled.

Back in my car, I roll up the windows, lock my doors, crank the AC. The woman alongside me glares and lays on her horn. Construction vehicles rumble to the sides. Workers holding flags and stop signs motion us forward. My voicemail pings. As traffic returns to multiple lanes, cars rocket past me. "Helen, this is Dan,

Gwen's husband. I found those pins. You're welcome to one. My wife says you're a regular. We're open 'til six."

I ignore the GPS's redirection and accelerate under clouds clearing off.

. . .

Rain never fell on me during my drive, but Shreveport's streets are soaked. Leaves and garbage are scattered about. Electric-company trucks cruise by, and one stops at a blank traffic light. Ladybug is dark when I roll in close to six. A handwritten sign on the door says POWER OUT BUT WE ARE OPEN – CASH ONLY.

"Gwen, hi. Helen Yager. I called about the pins."

She squints while leaning over a flashlight and sets down her can of almonds on the counter filled with shadows and dim shapes. "Oh, you made it." She dusts off her hands and pushes up her glasses.

"Is Dan here?"

"Let me get hold of him. He had to run out and help our daughter and son-in-law." She texts after her phone rings for a bit. "How was your drive?"

My ear buzzes. "Couldn't get here fast enough."

"That system picked up some steam. No tornadoes or flash floods like last time. Just a burst of rain and wind."

"Doesn't take much when it's quick."

Two customers emerge from the back, cradling old jackets, shawls, and trousers. They check some items before reaching the front.

"Find something?" Gwen pops almonds.

"We did. Thank you. How much is the mirror with the vines around it?"

"No price on it?"

The young women shake their heads no.

"Let me check."

"Your phone," I say as it buzzes on the counter.

Gwen returns with a blank price tag. "Our system is down, but…" She retrieves from under the register one of Mr. Carl's ledgers. Her phone buzzes. "Been a while since that mirror has seen the light of day." She stops on a line before flipping to another page. "I can't find it. How about one-hundred?"

The dark-haired girl's nose scrunches at her friend who mumbles about a budget.

"Do you mind if we look at it again?"

"Do you want help getting it down?"

I turn to the two young women. "Can you get it without her?"

"Yay!" Gwen says when the power clicks on.

"Your phone buzzed while you were helping them."

"That was our property manager asking about the security system. Let me try Dan again."

"Did he drop off the pins? Maybe he set one out for me?"

"Hey, Helen Yager is here. No? OK. The power's back. How's it goin'?" Gwen grabs some almonds.

The buzzing in my ear picks up.

"How late? We can have leftovers when you're back. OK, see you tonight." Gwen hangs up. "He says he never got over to storage, but he knows where the box is. Very easy to get to."

"I called and called you."

"He can get it tomorrow afternoon after three. We close at five but can stay around for you. He's tied up in Home Depot right now with everyone else because of a blackout."

"I'm leaving early tomorrow to be back for my shift."

"I apologize. If I had the key, I'd take you. Is there something else here you'd like instead?"

The two young women lower the mirror. Their fingerprints multiply all over the surface. Mr. Carl wore gloves when he handled items. He treated everything in the store as expensive, even the things that should have stayed in attics and basements. I turn from the front counter and toward the toy area where Mother found a puzzle—a wood triangle with holes for small wood pegs. "We used rusted horseshoe nails and a block about this big that jimmied up the tractor's flats," she said, her fingers too crooked to extend. She struggled jumping a peg over a peg like mud had stiffened her wrists. Her hearing faded, she moved about with her room's handrails, and she could only read a large-print daily devotion under which sat the triangle puzzle. We played every time I visited her. I can count on one hand when I won, reducing the pegs down to one. She didn't win much, but many attempts brought her closer. "Doesn't matter if you're getting buds or waiting on the weather," she said. "You got to suffer like land does."

. . .

When I reach my hotel room, my stomach is as grumpy as my ear, feet, and knuckles. Heat and humidity from sitting in my car has worsened, and they cling to me after I drag in my tired self and overnight bag. I eat my dinner as I kick off my shoes and, perched in the chair, rub my legs swollen from ankles to kneecaps. The room faces the sun, housecleaning did not close the curtains or turn on the AC, and my nachos' guacamole and sour cream, sitting too long in the sack and passenger seat, means I'll finish the evening with a nightcap of travel-size Milk of Magnesia.

"I do have something for her, and I want to stop by tonight," I tell Agee's after they answer their phone. "Thank you. I'll see you then."

Gwen's note in the box lays atop packing peanuts and tissue paper protecting the toy puzzle.

Helen,

Dan and I extend our deepest apologies to you for any miscommunication. We hope your mom likes this. We're hoping our grandkids will appreciate these old toys too, but they sure do love their video games. Please visit us again. We love seeing you and your mom in Ladybug.

One peg, green paint faded and scuffed, falls on the table. I wipe my fingers and roll it in my palm. It's like a miniature version of farm stakes Mother told me about—the kind driven into the ground for shoots to cling to. And, she laughed, no matter how many coats her family painted them to look different than fruits and vegetables, the camouflage never kept away rodents and bugs. Anything driven into the ground was more than the ground's and, like her, hid nothing and held back nothing.

"See these notches?" The man tapped a side.

I set down the two goat-milk jugs we found at the back of the store where Mr. Carl placed larger items. Mother glared at the man who angled his briefcase higher.

"She was supposed to reach Normandy but ended up servicing ships in the Channel. A U-Boat got her near the cliffs of Dover. She didn't sink. Just floated on her damage. The waves slapped her back, then out, then harder back to shore. Ever seen those cliffs?"

"Photos," Mr. Carl replied, taking out his jeweler's eyepiece.

"You can see where the torpedo scuffed it up. The numbers imprinted here denote its manufacturing date and foundry north of London." The man unfurled a white handkerchief and polished the side he had touched. He slid a piece of paper over the counter. "I've been quoted these numbers. Big range, but this one works for me." His ring with a red stone and gold weave flashed behind the circled dollar sign.

"Grandma Mabel had one of those," Mother mumbled. "Costume jewelry." Her bones and skin were her brittle parts then. But her memory cut like a whistle across fields.

The man half smiled at us before focusing again on Mr. Carl. "I'm willing to take twenty percent off." His ring flashed again when his pen scribbled a new number next to the circle. "The sixty-fifth anniversary of World War II is right around the corner. The markets are getting hot."

"I know," said Mr. Carl.

"This can be your first piece. First of many once word gets out." The man checked his watch. "I have a meeting with another interested party in an hour. What time do you close today?"

"Don't." Mother leaned her body toward Mr. Carl. She scolded the air—the joints in her fingers like walnuts. "That's from a cotton baler."

The man said, "I beg your pardon."

"My father got his hand crunched in one."

The man's eyes returned to Mr. Carl who crossed his arms.

"And my brother has a shed full of those from the farm he turns into art."

"Maybe he should sell them."

"That's not why he does it. But you're trying to make money from a stack of bull so high you can smell it across county lines."

The man's jawline bristled. He swept the items into his briefcase and fled the store.

. . .

A small band of sunset breaks up evening when I reach Agee's. They are as kind in person as they've been on the phone. I hand the peg to them. I tell them I'll be back next week or, if they need, earlier. I put my car in gear and reach the end of their property—a lane long enough for a hearse and anyone following it. Mother's cremation will be a small gathering. Everyone one on her side has either passed on or is too frail to travel. It may be only me.

I circle back to the office. Tom, the son, steps back out. I tell him I made a mistake. One small but important change. Please. He nods, saying, Of course—what can we do? Mother's hands should not be by her side as I wanted. They should be over her heart. One hand holding the peg close to her. The other on top like a prayer. I ask him if it's too late. No, he says.

Body Bearers

The truck chugs up and down hills rolling across sunrise and tilts for the workshop at the back where flowers and tall grass separate mounds of wood and metal; hoists and levers; generators; wheels and axles; benches and seats; and wagons, buggies, and carriages from the driveway along the two-story house, paint-flecked and summer-soaked, from which two boys sprint—one jumping over puddles and yelling, "Come on, Shaw!"; the other examining the water—and rush into the workshop where Clarence, coffee and flashlight on the desk, bends over the finishing touches on the funeral caisson.

Inside, under the front lip and between driver and passenger seats, where gold strips wrap the frame and contrast the navy satin shining on the body, Clarence applies the decal of laurels and birth and death dates. He drags the heat gun across the decal until bubbles flatten, ready for a quick-drying sealant he brushes over when Benjamin yells, "Grandad, they're here!"

Brakes squeak, the truck shivers to a stop, and Marines slide out one by one. The commanding officer waves to Clarence who waves back and snatches his cane.

"Good morning, Mr. DeWare."

Clarence welcomes the commanding officer while glancing at the name tag. "No Captain Till today?"

"No, sir. He's been reassigned."

"Hope he's not in trouble."

Boyer only nods at the tease.

"Well, tell him I said hi and we missed him today."

"Yes, sir." Boyer inspects the caisson. "We ready to go?"

"Just finished up." Clarence massages his knuckles and elbow swelling under his charcoal skin.

Boyer motions to his detail, one of whom reverses the truck until its bed faces the caisson where his men load and secure it—strapped down and wheels locked—before they drape it, raise the truck's back cover, and signal that the caisson won't snag on its way in. They handle it like something sturdy but temporal and designed for carrying something fragile and eternal.

A private motions to Boyer who motions back; the Marines file into the truck rumbling alive.

After leaning through the passenger-side window, Boyer passes an envelope to Clarence. "Thank you again."

"Of course. See you soon."

The two men shake hands, and as Boyer climbs in, the truck grinds into drive, and Benjamin and Shaw wave to the soldiers who wave as the truck inches toward the gate.

Clarence reads the embossed letter and, stopping halfway, quickly creases it. "Damn," he mutters. "You gotta be kidding me." His eyes strain following his grandsons who—Benjamin forging ahead; Shaw pausing at spots as he dawdles behind—

shadow the truck until it returns to the county road leading to the highway and the silence it came from and brought.

"That was fast."

Clarence's gray head turns toward his wife.

"How's Captain Till?"

Clarence jabs at the paper he tossed on the desk; Shoshanna unfolds it.

Dear Mr. DeWare,

Yearly budget appraisals and recent financial constraints require the Corps to reevaluate contracts and contractors. As such, and as difficult as these decisions are, we will not be renewing your contract for Marine Corps Body Bearers.

Thank you for your service to the Corps and its Ceremonial Memorial division. We wish you nothing but the best with your future endeavors. Should you have any questions…

"This came out of nowhere," she says.

"I bet it's a computer doing it for them now."

She rubs his chest. "I'm sorry."

Benjamin skids across sawdust and copper spirals. "Beat you again!"

Shaw sweats and gasps. "Granma, can I have some milk?"

"I bet Grandaddy's got some." Her glasses motion toward the refrigerator alongside the workshop's garage.

The two boys share a bottle and, when it's empty, add it to the stack by an old pickup branded DEWARE BUGGYS, CARRIAGES & WAGONS – HOLLER RIDGE, VA.

"It's time to take those in," Benjamin says, spinning in a chair. "We made enough last time to get cupcakes from the bakery."

"I'm gonna need more than fiber today." Clarence chuckles before frowning. "And we're gonna need more than what bottles can get us."

"We'll get you one too, Granma."

"If you bring some blueberries back, I'll make us a batch."

Benjamin fishes for keys on a pegboard.

"Do you want help?" Shaw's voice softens.

Clarence jangles the keys. "There's nothing left to do here."

• • •

After the boys scamper into the store and drool over bins and family-size tubs of ice cream, Benjamin opens doors in the frozen aisles and Shaw closes them; and they gag when they slide into the section of alternative meats. Clarence toddles behind, making sure nothing will melt or be taste-tested. He says no to their armful of boxes—one of which, Shaw notes, is two-for-one; and Clarence holds up one finger when the boys return from a shelf and juggle treats. Benjamin swings his waist until he decides on a caramel-drizzled ice-cream sandwich, and Shaw, sitting cross-legged on the tile, debates if red or purple sprinkles would be better as puddles after they melt on the sidewalks.

"Get both," Clarence says. "But you split one with your brother."

"I will. I promise."

"And get one for me."

The boys jump in place.

"But don't eat till we're done." Clarence lifts the shopping basket for their treats. "And now for some blueberries and flour."

"This way!" Charging ahead, Benjamin turns right for produce.

"I know where the flour is," Shaw says. "And I know which one Granma likes."

"OK. We're all depending on you. We can't have blueberry muffins without flour."

"You can't have blueberry muffins without blueberries."

"This is also true." Clarence grimaces when apples spill onto the floor in the distance. "Meet us in checkout."

Shaw pauses at a rack of toys and coloring books and checks with Clarence who approves before heading for the apples. Shaw selects four things and walks to the baking section.

"These aren't blueberries." Clarence stops another apple pyramid from flattening as Benjamin tugs the middle.

"We don't have these in the shop. Granma says an apple a day is good for you."

"They'll rot and make things worse."

"Bugs are already in there."

"They came with everything."

"But you eat out there."

"I put my trash away. Seal it up before any critters get it." Clarence's back locks up when he helps an employee clean up the spilled apples. "Throw any of the bruised ones in there." He winces pointing his cane at his shopping basket. "I'll pay for them."

"No, it's OK," the employee replies. "Thank you though."

"May I for a sec?"

"Sure."

Clarence rests on a ladder between lettuce and cabbage. "Benjy…as I was saying, I can sweep away crumbs, but juice is something else. Anything sticky out in the shop ruins what I've worked on."

"Didn't you build one for Mom and Dad?" Benjamin asks, raising a stem of blueberries.

Clarence freezes when a white cloud puffs above a register where Shaw struggles picking up the flour sack he dropped. Clarence has Benjamin carry and unload the basket and help

Shaw. The price glows on the screen; Clarence mentions to the cashier he forgot something. He and the boys roll a shopping cart to the parking lot and parallel it along the pickup's gate, where Benjamin, skittering about, jokes he could be faster if he had an apple, and Shaw directs where the milk bottles should go—the glass holding nothing but the breeze whistling over them.

They reenter the store, navigating corners and customers, and turn for their cashier who, after counting, offers cash or the difference subtracted from the bill.

"That's at least a dozen muffins," Clarence says.

The boys' eyes bug out.

"But not today."

As they exit the store, they take turns steering the cart and unwrapping their goodies.

"Come on, Grandad."

The boys slurp, lick their lips and fingers, and reach the pickup before Clarence who stops at a sign by the manager's office: HIRING ALL POSITIONS – APPLY WITHIN.

* * *

When they return home, Shoshanna asks, "Did you hit the jackpot?"

"Discount," the boys say, setting the muffin ingredients on the kitchen table.

She stretches her apron and wipes their faces. "Looks like Grandad fed you a morning snack." She glances out the window at Clarence wheezing after parking the pickup and walking toward the back door.

Shaw lines the four toys on the table; points to the robot for Benjamin who runs outside with it before running back in, saying thank you, rushing back outside, and saving the planet; lifts the flowers, no bigger than dimes, to Shoshanna who mouths *Thank you* and returns to the mixing bowl; adds the new crayon box to his art bin; and offers the tiny treasure chest to Clarence whose growl crumbles into a groan when he sits.

Clarence waits until Shaw, grabbing his art bin and sketchpad, joins Benjamin in the backyard. "Tysons is hiring."

"You're exhausted from going there," Shoshanna says, divvying out blueberries.

"Earlier knocked me off." He struggles opening the chest.

"We'll be OK for a while. I'll have my pension in a few years."

Clarence pulls back the lid—empty. "Which doesn't help right now. We've talked about their college or whatever they want we can help with. And if we pull from our retirement early…"

"If you work there, you may not come back at all."

"It'll be easier than here."

"You control a lot here. Your work. Your breaks."

"Not anymore." After Clarence fumbles setting one of Shoshanna's toy flowers in the chest, he closes the lid and scoots the tiny flower in front of the chest like a red wax seal fallen off. "John got that greeting-job at Walmart. And Dolores helped that accountant to cover expenses after surgery."

"Which is exactly what'll happen." She stops dicing butter. "If you die or hobble up before we get unstuck, I'll have to work there."

"You'll end up seeing all your DMV customers in the headache aisle."

They laugh. Clarence brushes off Shoshanna's help when he stands and wobbles on his cane. They embrace each other while standing at the kitchen window. The boys fade in and out of shadows and among half-complete, to-be-recycled, and abandoned parts.

Clarence calls the boys over when he and Shoshanna walk to the workshop. He peels back a tarp covering a buggy secluded at the back, under an extra roof protecting it from weather, and raised on concrete blocks—a room with three walls and cloth sheets for doors. He pats two circular spaces on the long purple bench between driver and passenger. "Your parents' urns fit right here. When I carved this out, I cried then laughed so hard I fell down and couldn't get up."

"I got home from work and saw him," Shoshanna says. "I thought he had a heart attack."

"'Look at that,' I said to Granma. 'It looks like a cup holder for coffee or a Coke.'"

"I laughed because he was right." She turns to the boys. "Your mom loved coffee no matter where she was off to."

"A milk bottle fits there," Shaw says.

Clarence and Shoshanna smile at him while Benjamin's robot defends the terrain.

"You know Mr. Aughton down the road? You've played with his grandson Billy when he visits."

The boys shake their heads yes.

"He let us borrow one of his horses. Granma sat next to me." Clarence drags his cane in the dirt.

"I remember that!" Benjamin bursts out.

Shaw swallows and falls quiet; his eyes float around the painted wood and soft interior framing a moment.

"We hitched the horse and headed out," Shoshanna says. "We dressed up like when we go to church."

Perking up, Shaw faintly says, "I remember that."

"Shaw lets me wear his ties." Benjamin wraps his arm around his brother.

"Everybody got a ride in the country before rain came."

"What a day to say goodbye." Shoshanna pats her forehead.

"Your daddy was my best employee."

"Shenay loved it, hated it, wanted out, came back, loved it again."

Clarence looks from Shaw to Benjamin. "It's not for the military. This one's ours." His hands run over the wheels. "One horse pulled this. But poor guy got stuck in the mud. We had to walk the rest of the way to the cemetery."

"You hopped out and tried to pull him," Shoshanna says, chuckling at Benjamin.

"I kinda remember that."

"You found a tree branch and hoped he wanted to eat it."

"I know better now. I needed carrots."

"Where was I?"

"You stayed sitting right between us." Clarence kisses Shaw's head. "You told the horse it was OK because none of it was his fault."

A breeze cuts through the workshop and pushes out the sheets marking the entrance and exit to the private shelter at the back, built around the buggy, and the breeze lifts the sheets long enough for something to come in or out—to carry off or leave behind—before it dies down and the sheets close around the weight that had been inside.

. . .

"My man, this seat's got your name on it." The manager's tone bounces along his office's wood-paneled walls like a gameshow host. His single bleached curl clings to his forehead. He raises a box of rainbow-sprinkle donuts. "Fresh today. Compliments of the chef." His pierced eyebrows bob. "Which could be you."

"I haven't baked since I helped my mother and grandmothers. I think I'd serve you better not in the bakery." Clarence's cane slumps to the armrest as he reaches for a donut. "But I'll eat it all up."

"Right on." Glichman hands a napkin to Clarence and stacks donuts for himself. "OK…not the bakery. We have openings in dairy, stocking and inventory, and meat and seafood. Any of that float your boat?"

"I've seen your delivery vans around town."

"Yeah you have." Glichman winks before cruising through his computer. "All our full-time mornings and afternoons are filled."

Clarence bites his bottom lip.

"But we have an evening spot. Six until eight. Weekdays." Glichman devours his second donut. "You get to keep your weekends."

"Only two hours?"

"It's one of our busiest times. People getting off work, not wanting to come in, want something delivered. If you do it right, it'll keep us going."

"Well…I'll take what you got."

"We want you to take what we got." Glichman offers a fist-bump, but Clarence fumbles through it and shakes hands. "Let me get some paperwork." He double-clicks his mouse; the printer whirs alive. "I started our deliveries. And its system."

"How long have you been here?"

"Like a never-ending dream."

The office door opens after a knock. "Brian?" A middle-aged woman cradles a scanner. "The honey hams aren't coming up as two-for-one. Mrs. Bedders is not happy."

Glichman types on his computer. "You and the morning team verified that yesterday, yes?"

"I thought so."

"That's a total bummer for Mrs. Bedders's Wednesday. And ours." Glichman stands—his desk no longer hiding his board shorts and the wind speeds and nautical paths dotting them—and hands an application to Clarence. From a bottom drawer he pulls out black slacks he slides over his Chuck Taylors and shorts. "Fill those out. I'll be back in two." He holds up his fingers not like a peace sign but like they're missing a joint for him to smoke. "Use the orange pen." He throws his bloodshot eyes at a wire basket on his desk. "It works for me."

After the office door closes, Clarence rolls over the pen: OUTER BANKS SUMMER CLASSIC – BREAKING WAVES & MAKING NAMES. A miniature surfer floats down the middle, chased by a shark, teeth flared, and thumps into a pier behind the nib. Clarence fills out his full name, date of birth, address and phone, and emergency contact, all of which, he sighs, takes him or anyone looking for or aiding him back to one person and one place—Shoshanna and the house but not to Shaw and Benjamin because they are too young. He pauses on

PREVIOUS POSITION and SUPERVISOR and sees the workshop holding twenty-seven of his sixty-one years; skills he developed under its roof and inside its walls after an office downsized its cubicles and let him go with little to hold or extend from; time soaked there with Shenay, who said she would return one day and help him manage the things he couldn't or didn't want to, and Wendell helping him build buggies and carriages for the living and wagons for the dead before preaching about being born again and remade new and whole; and materials scattered about the shop floor before he prepared them. *As soon as possible* he adds to EARLIEST DATE AVAILABLE. On the last page, Clarence signs his name and tips the pen the other way. The surfer pursues the retreating shark.

"Got it squared away?" Clarence asks Glichman after he returns.

"Mrs. Bedders will take home two honey hams. But…" Glichman punches the keyboard. "On us."

Clarence passes over his application. "Maybe I can deliver it to her so she doesn't have to worry about coming in."

"My man, you're thinking the way you need to think here." Glichman slides off his slacks but, as the wall clock approaches noon, pulls from the desk's bottom drawer a belt and cartoon-carrot tie. "Come in at five-thirty tomorrow."

"Will do." Clarence leans on his cane and stands up. "Thank you."

. . .

Suds overflow the sink as the boys squeeze a bottle whenever Clarence shuffles to the table and collects dishes and silverware; they feign innocence when he peeps over his shoulder at them. Shoshanna throws napkins in a laundry basket and wraps dinner in foil—the boys receiving more chicken, mashed potatoes, and green beans than her and Clarence as well as small containers of blueberry cobbler she baked after the muffins; she writes on the outside which grandson gets which, adding X's and O's. She tells them they can stay up until eight-thirty if they clean better than last time—Shaw washing; Benjamin drying—and teases them, if they don't, they'll have to get jobs until school starts to pay for all the wasted soap and water or if the dishes end up like the one she pulls from the cabinet and flicks off dried food.

"We'll go to work with you every day," Benjamin says, stacking plates as though they can't chip or crack. "I'll bring a lunch and coffee. I won't ever take a smoke break."

Clarence's cane slides a large knife, next in line, away from Benjamin.

"Don't you remember when you visited me?" Shoshanna asks.

"I do!" Shaw shakes his head before whispering in Benjamin's ear.

The boys intone, "Next number. Ding! Ding! Ding!" Their soapy hands pull their faces down like they're melting.

"Sorry, Granma. No can do. We'll work for Grandad."

"I can make the stickers, and Benjamin can nail-gun them in place."

"We can make the wheels, Shaw."

The boys ooh and ahh, spinning their heads; they click their tongues. A fork bounces on the floor between them; Clarence straddles picking it up.

"You'll be working for free," he says.

"Did you pay Mom and Dad?"

"In room and Granma's food. Besides, ministers need to learn about ascetic living."

Shoshanna says, "There's nothing wrong with doing the most with less."

"What's *ascetic* mean?"

Clarence says to Shaw, "It means you remove everything you think you need."

"Like before they died and went to heaven?"

Clarence shifts on his cane in front of Shaw before Benjamin pulls him away with "We're done! Let's go!"

"No TV. It's Wednesday," Shoshanna says when the boys run into the living room. After confirming they shuffle through the book and puzzle shelves, she fills a kettle while Clarence stuffs ice cubes into a sandwich bag and slides it onto his back. "Tired?"

"Yesterday is catching up with me. I wanted to get it done before they showed up."

"You did."

"I wish I'd known what my effort would get for it." Clarence stares into the living room and at the shadows jumping back and forth as sunset glows along the horizon. "I want to talk to you about Tysons."

"Me too."

The kettle whistles, and Shoshanna tops off two mugs as Clarence and his cane navigate the living room rug where Benjamin plays and Shaw draws. He sinks into his chair and flicks on the radio. Shoshanna, on the sofa, her feet propped on an ottoman, opens a magazine. A small circular table between them holds their teas; photos of Shenay and Wendell graduating from seminary, exchanging vows, and missionary work in inner cities and Appalachia—Shenay teaching in a classroom; Wendell, with one of Clarence's old hammers, hoisting roofing materials to a building's top; and photos of Benjamin swinging in a Little League batter's box and younger Shaw sharing his drawing of a sled above which the sun's rays pull the sled to a gate atop a valley.

"That was 'Camino Solitario'…'Lonely Road,' by Fernando Gomez, considered one of Spain's master contemporary acoustic guitarists," the radio host says.

Benjamin strides his robot across taped-together papers and their galaxies, planets, and stars Shaw illustrated. At the end of the drawing, near a purple spiral, two spaceships float. Two children aboard the smaller ship smile as it approaches the larger one where a man and a woman inside open the door and operate levers extending from the hull toward the smaller ship.

"Next up 'If I Should Fall Behind' by…"

Shoshanna flips a page. "What would you do there?"

"They have something I can do."

She looks at him through steam.

Benjamin searches for the other toys from the store because Shaw misplaced them and worries they won't be found. "It's OK," Benjamin says. "I'll get them." After he does, he shows them to Shaw who sets the flowers under the woman in the larger spaceship and the treasure chest under the man.

"It will be a while until my pension, and orders here….who knows?"

"I'll get something, but not like it was. Not through the military."

Benjamin sets the robot amid the celebration and rotates its arms and torso to welcome the reunited travelers.

"You should do it."

Clarence snaps toward Shoshanna.

"They'll outlive us," she says.

"They have to." The bottom of Clarence's cane double taps the wood floor. "I already did it anyway."

Her grin matches his. "I knew you were up to something earlier today. Is that where you went by yourself?"

"I told you I had to run to town for some errands." Aided by his cane, his chest puffs. "I'll be delivering groceries. Probably to old folks like us and everyone we know."

"Don't do anything asking too much of you over there, or we'll have to come get your body and slide you onto something you made."

He peers at her over his mug and glasses. "Still can, if I ever have to."

. . .

On its way out of the lot, the red van honks to Glichman standing under a canopy, clipboard in one hand and tablet in the other, and honks again when Clarence waves and walks over to the green van with a grocery bag fanning out a rainbow and racing toward the phone number, website, and puffy TYSONS GROCERIES.

"That was Ahn. Super-great, super-chill guy. Needs to be a little less assuming about tips from customers and way better with time management. But his wife makes the best pho. And I've been to Vietnam. But hers was more bliss than anything I was on over there." Glichman hands a print-off to Clarence. "I'll have us paperless soon. You know how owners can be." After flipping between paper and digital content, Glichman turns on his tablet's stopwatch.

"Stuck in their ways." Clarence adjusts his glasses and store-branded shirt and ball cap.

"I have, like, zero patience for that." Glichman slaps and opens the driver's door. "I've been working on the COO to get two more. Took me three years for these and our tech tweaks. I said, 'Larry, the future is before the present, and if we don't strike, it will pass us by. Our comps are ahead of us. Do you want to be them or be Tysons?' After we got bought out, I didn't have to ride as hard."

Clarence sets his cane in the passenger seat and, gripping the steering wheel and driver-side armrest, climbs in. When he finds the lumbar-support button, he maxes it out. His arthritis burns when he grips the steering wheel.

"Man!" Glichman whistles, stepping back. "You are looking ready for your first go. I looked half as good as you when I was back there." He checks his tablet's stopwatch. "Some real-quick things." He highlights an address on Clarence's roster. "Serious vampire-suck of an intersection here. Especially during rush hour. You wouldn't think so given it's near a school for the blind and deaf. The previous guy got t-boned big time, ended up in Critical."

"That's too bad."

"He lied to us about his driving record. Cost us a lot. Including my reputation." Glichman taps a name lines down. "This family has super-cute fluffballs, but they bark every time we're there, which brings out this cat lady. She was off her meds the day I filled in after firing the guy you're replacing. She said to me, 'Ford or Chevy?' I said, 'Subaru,' which sent her cackling back inside." He checks the stopwatch. "Raul will wheel out your goods, I'll run through any last-minute Q's you have, and you can catch the wind." Before Glichman disappears behind the van, he swivels a shaka.

"Am I to help with loading?" Clarence twists the rearview mirror, and when silence answers him, he leans out the window. Heavy strips of plastic swing in the doorway of the store's backside; silhouettes move behind them in concert with coaster squeaks.

The van's cargo and rear doors fly open, and the summer evening erases blocks of darkness behind Clarence while a short bald man returns inside with a cart. As Clarence slides from the seat, and before he can grab his cane, his back twists. He hunches over; the jolt knocks out his breath. Purple spreads from his peripheries, and a horizon rocks up in one eye and rolls down in his other. One of his knees drops to the pavement, and he balances against a tire. The purple breaks, light caught between day and evening floods Clarence, and he hovers over the pallet of bags. Loading the first bag worsens his back, and tinnitus smothers the sounds of his loading the remaining ones. Resting on his knees, the pallet emptied and van filled, he stops at the cab. His leg freezes; pain shoots along his hip, hamstring, and under his ribs. He hobbles into the store, the door-strips smacking him, and braces himself on a shelf.

Glichman breaks through customers who stop, stare, and mumble. "You need to stay in the back." He fakes a smile to Clarence and everyone else. "There's a buzzer you push when you need me."

"My back's locked up. I can't go."

Glichman closes the door.

"I'll rest it real good tonight and be back tomorrow."

"Tomorrow…OK." Glichman checks something on his tablet and swipes away a screen. "Don't forget to clock out. And as a new employee, you're on probation for thirty days, and I'll have to mark this in your file. I hate doing this, but you have a warning. Two warnings is suspension." He tracks down Raul who takes the keys and drives off in the van.

Clarence buys a water and extra-strength aspirin from the front, where customers wait, and broods in his pickup. When his watch ticks after 8:15, he heads home where the boys, before bedtime, hug him, tell him about their day—Shaw sketching with colored pencils and rulers from the workshop; Benjamin, armed with his baseball bat, vanquishing a swamp monster slithering among tarps—and show him the "s'ghetti and meatballs" they saved for him. He cries reaching for the dish at the back of the refrigerator.

"How was it?" Shoshanna asks, tightening her robe.

He chews slowly and swallows. "Rinse and repeat for tomorrow. How was your day?"

"Steady." She stares at him while he quivers in his chair.

. . .

Glichman smiles like a salesman while Clarence and Raul unload bags from the cart and load them in the van. "Back around and stronger the second time."

"My mother taught us the sun rises the next day," Clarence says, falling behind Raul's pace but positioning himself for the largest and last bag before his shorter, leaner, agile coworker can.

Glichman checks a tag. "The Watooshis got their pizzas and gummy worms for movie night. What do you guess it'll be?"

"I hope something they all like. Fills them up as a family," Clarence replies, coughing. Sweat stains his shirt as he drags his leg near the van's side before he finds his cane.

Staring at Clarence, Raul says, "They live on Park. It's probably shit NPR loves." His bald head glistens under the overhead light by the loading dock when he fist-bumps Glichman.

Glichman clicks the lap button on his tablet's stopwatch after Raul heads into the store and cuts through the door-strips like they're paper. "He made so much extra in tips last night, came back before Ahn's run, finished his inside duties, *and* pitched in with overnight stocking for about an hour. Left after midnight.

Overtime for us? Solid worth." He hands the list to Clarence. "He took his evening break out here so Ahn could see him. How much knife sharpening can you do in front of the wounded?"

Forcing a smile, Clarence shifts in his seat as it digs into his kidney.

"Super clear-cut tonight. Fridays are usually like this." Glichman checks the stopwatch running past Raul's time.

Clarence starts the van and clips the list alongside the steering wheel. "My mother also used to say, 'Hands are better for helping, not holding down.'"

"Be back before eight." A screen pops up on Glichman's tablet. "New employees can't have overtime until your probation is done." Dolphins tattooed on his fingers resting on the driver-side window spring from waves drawn like barbed wire.

"I'll be back before you know I was ever gone." Clarence scans the list. As he puts the van in gear, he recognizes the last stop's name and chuckles about how small the town is.

After he completes more than half the list, faster than he anticipated, save for three flaws—a misheard entry code to a gate where the line behind him grew and honked; a woman asking for the name of his supervisor because last week's tilapia did not last as long in her fridge as a competitor's; and a hubcap and tire rub on a curb he misjudged—he stops, stretches, and tops off the gas tank. He pulls into a gas station across from the burger-and-shakes joint he, Shoshanna, and the boys went to. As the pump clicks on, he counts his tips, hums while dancing his neck and shoulders to the victory in his head, leans his cane against the van, and stands without swaying, tipping over, or tensing until Shaw's voice asking "What does that mean?" stabs him. His arms splay for his cane and slap the door. A customer across the island looks up from washing her windshield. Clarence smiles but not at her.

"It means Grandad and I take care of you now," Shoshanna answered while Benjamin comforted Shaw. "Your mom and dad said so in a piece of paper."

"No," Shaw mumbled. "Why didn't those bags save them? I've seen them in a video. All those cars have them."

Clarence slid his remaining fries to the boys and filled their cups with the milkshake he did not drink. He and Shoshanna held hands under the table. "Things like that don't always work."

"You should add it to your stuff you build," Shaw said. "No one would lose anyone ever."

Benjamin nodded. "Yeah, they should have been in one of your wagons."

Clarence calms himself in the van, consults his list, folds the gas receipt, and drives to an area similar to his but on the opposite side of the county and far from the store. He parks behind an SUV blocking the rest of the way to the house. After wielding the handcart down a long walkway, every stone tipping or stalling it, he rubs his back before knocking on the front door. A man around Clarence's age answers.

"Mr. Stohup?"

"Yes."

The two men stare at each other.

"I have your grocery delivery."

"Fantastic."

Clarence cringes, setting the groceries inside the foyer.

"Thank you." Stohup leans over. "I'll help you next time."

"The boss wouldn't like that."

"He runs a too-tight ship?"

"He can swim if it sinks."

The two men laugh.

"Thank you for using our service." Clarence unstraps his cane from the handcart. "Enjoy your night. Maybe I'll see you next week."

As Clarence heads back, Stohup steps closer. "I think you built a buggy for my daughter when she was young."

"You looked familiar to me too."

"She loved that thing."

"Good. I loved making it for her. How she doing?"

"She's a busy mom, and she's so great with it all."

"It's a lot to juggle."

"It sure is." Stohup glances at the van and a dairy bottle, meats, vegetables, and fruits stitched on Clarence's shirt. "You still do it?"

"I do."

"We've got grandkids. Carolyn's. They need something that sits in place. Could you make one like it needs a horse but doesn't?"

"Sure."

"A toy like that would be good. Smaller than the one you made for Carolyn." Stohup shrinks a space as though its size is a small heart. "Just sitting there for them."

"I'd love to make that." Clarence pulls out a tattered business card from his wallet and, with the clipboard's pen, strikes through the workshop phone number and writes in the house. "If I don't answer, my wife or grandsons will."

"I'll be in touch." Stohup offers a tip.

Clarence waves him off. "I'll hear from you soon."

After the last two stops, he pulls into the back lot after eight and parks next to the other van, his pickup the only employee vehicle, and the dark quiet surprises him. Few headlights in the front lot flash on and streak by; customers come and go from the store, but compared to the earlier rush, they trickle and disappear as quickly as they appear. No coworker greets him after he enters the store through the back. The soft-keyboard playlist on the overhead speakers walks with him as he passes aisles, carts squeaking and registers ringing in the distance, and DANGER WET FLOOR signs fencing an area. He hooks his work shirt in his locker in the employee break room—the tables and chairs empty; lights off—but then retrieves it and folds it over his arm for a wash at home. He clocks out and drops the van keys in the box outside Glichman's office.

"You're late."

Clarence shuffles into the doorway.

"Why did you get gas?" Glichman refers to a screen on his tablet.

"It was almost empty."

"Did you pay for it?"

"I figured you'd reimburse me."

"We'll bake that into your day when it's time for you to get gas. Cool?"

Clarence nods.

"That tank is on you." Glichman flips to another screen. A van icon above IN and OUT and MILEAGE pulses on a road turned red in the middle of green. "You stayed at the Stohups's residence longer than needed."

"We know each other."

"More than groceries?"

"Is that a problem?"

"Groceries out and back. That's it."

"Got it," Clarence mutters, tensing on his cane. "I'll see you Monday."

"I got to give you your second warning." Glichman scoots his chair to his desktop computer where he continues typing.

"For what?" Clarence snaps. "Getting gas? Talking to someone I know?"

"You're suspended until the end of your probation. We'll reassess then."

• • •

The master is the only bright room when Clarence walks into the quiet house resembling the store. Game-night popcorn lingers in the kitchen, and the refrigerator has a bowl of it alongside meatloaf and carrots and a note from Shoshanna and the boys, but he pours a bourbon and drops into a chair at the table holding tallies from rounds of Monopoly. The evening, he imagines, went smoothly until the boys, losing on their own against their Granma, joined forces and bent rules, blatantly in front of her, if they had to, like he and Shenay whenever they were losing to Shoshanna. And when Shenay married Wendell, we all had to gang up on him, Clarence recalls, chuckling to his glass and heading upstairs.

He opens the boys' door and mouths *I love you* while race cars and stars on the ceiling glow and the mobile between the boys' beds pivots its circus animals, Ferris wheel, and roller-coaster cars the way it did when it hung for Shenay.

"Hi there," Shoshanna says after Clarence enters the master bedroom. "How was it?"

"Did you happen to get a phone call tonight from a Dennis Stohup?"

"No."

"Maybe his daughter called?"

"Sorry."

"Did the boys answer the phone when you weren't looking?"

She closes her book. "My cell rang, but it was a telemarketer."

He shuffles to the closet while the noise in his head worsens. "How was your day?"

"Only four people blew up at me, including the mother of a teenage girl who missed her permit test by two points. Everyone else was pissed they didn't have the right documents and let us know we should clarify that on the website. Which we have. But this was all before lunch. Made the afternoon better."

He holds up his work shirt before throwing it in the laundry basket; the sweat-smile collapses into itself. "I got my second warning tonight." His flops onto the bed. "I'm suspended."

"Second warning?" She peers at their door leading to the hall and the boys' room.

"My back got so bad I couldn't even start work." His cane wedges into his shoes and pops them off. "Didn't get paid enough for that."

"What happened?"

"I wasn't fast and efficient." He finds his slippers and bathrobe. "Some machine says it's right, but I'm not? And that manager? He thinks he'll push himself into a business suit and a corporate office." He stares at crops across the road, the moon highlighting them inside black fields, and grinds his cane into the rug. "I hope the machines he gave them take his job away."

"What happens next?"

"I can be back there. And not earn bad marks." Clarence heads for the bathroom.

"That's not good long- or short-term."

"But none of this now or in the future will be getting any cheaper."

Clarence looks at the phone on his nightstand. Steam billows in the bathroom as the shower runs. He focuses on the phone while he sits on the tub's edge, drops his feet in one by one, and moving no further, waits like a jar to be filled.

● ● ●

Their sneakers sliding on the gravel outside the workshop, the boys yell, "Granma's ready!"

Clarence peeks behind him from his desk computer blinking and buzzing under papers, manuals, cobwebs, and dust. He tells the boys he's just about done. He searches for *Stohup* and *Dennis* —and misfiling or misspellings—which brings up *Lt. Gen. Max Dennis* and his Arlington interment eleven years ago and *D. Ennis Rodgers* in Staunton and her request for modified designs for an auction benefitting special-needs riders; through decades-old orders; a date or wagon or buggy models attached to memories of young Shenay or Wendell helping him or the boys playing in snow while he worked past sunset or stopped in the middle of work because of a thunderstorm; blueprints and works-in-progress images; reports; and tax filings Shoshanna and the boys digitized last summer. He scrolls, stops, scrolls.

Shaw says, "We have to take her car because your pickup is too small for all of us."

"We can squeeze in there." Clarence opens his email and scans folders. "We used to."

"When we were teeny-tiny." Shaw's voice pitches up as he holds pebble-sized Benjamin and him.

"She has the better radio." Benjamin opens and closes file cabinets down from Clarence's desk.

"I don't know about that. Her tastes aren't anywhere near my standards."

Shaw blushes. "Yours are pretty low."

"Are you telling me her tunes are better?"

"We know her stuff."

"Yeah, she sings along." Benjamin rolls an embossed paper into a trumpet.

"I sing along when we're together."

"You sing like those old barbershop singers."

"A little off the top. Please and thank you, sir."

Clarence takes scissors away from Benjamin before he cuts Shaw's hair.

"Ready?"

Clarence pivots in his chair at Shoshanna. The boys run for the car's backseat and buckle up; their cheering reverberates in the workshop.

"What are you doing?"

Clarence turns off the monitor. "I hadn't turned this on for a few days."

She pauses before dangling her keys. "Drive or ride?"

"Ride. Everything about me could use a break."

After Shoshanna leaves the workshop, Clarence checks the drawer Benjamin did not close. He cruises through the Q's and R's and slows through the S's. A long car honk scares him. The boys' laughter pierces his heart. His back creaks when he stands up. He sets one file on the desk before making his way to the car.

"I want to go down to the pond."

"We went there last Saturday, Shaw. What if we went on the road between here and wherever?"

"No destination?" Clarence asks.

Benjamin's head iterates yes; Shaw's no. They giggle and switch answers.

Shoshanna finds a song the boys like. She asks Clarence, "Did you find what you were looking for?"

"Yeah. When I need it."

The car jiggles over rocky patches in the road, but when it hits smoother sections, Clarence's knees keep shimmying. Songs come and go, and in the silences between them, the boys hum or chant their favorite melodies and lyrics while Clarence peers out the window. The landscape flies by with summer greens, streams, thick grass and trees—a spreading-out far, wide, and deep like wishes.

Reaching over, Shoshanna faintly sings to Clarence.

"Fall will be here before you know it," he says.

"New clothes. New shoes." She glimpses in the rearview mirror as a long stretch, the tires' drone, and a blue sky soften the boys until their voices fade and they fall asleep. "Shaw will want a new computer."

"He wants one every year. I heard him tell Benjamin, 'I'll sell you my old one.'"

"He what?"

"He said, 'That money you made mowing the church lawn I'll take only ten percent for it.'"

Shoshanna covers her mouth after laughing out loud. The boys slump a little more in the backseat—Shaw snoring; Benjamin drooling.

"But," Clarence continues, "Benjy came back with 'How 'bout you give it to me *or* you share it with me, and I won't tell Granma and Grandad or Pastor John about the books you haven't returned to the church library. Aren't you up to about seven now?'"

"What'd Shaw say?"

"You know how he is with that. 'Well…I…God wants me to be this. God gave you other talents like sports to be good at.'"

"They're just like Shenay."

"It's like we got half Shenay over here and half over there." Clarence divides a life hanging in the air. He snaps toward his window when a bouquet of flowers and, in a ditch by a blind curve bending behind rocks and trees, a cardboard cross and its painted-on date pass by. "Somebody lost someone there."

"Joel told me so many people have asked County to fix it."

"I may be shift manager at Tysons by the time that happens." Shoshanna makes a face.

"And then I can buy them all the computers and books. Pay off our mortgages. Their college tuitions. And still have enough for us and their inheritance."

"I can kiss the DMV goodbye."

"I can line up this whole fleet of delivery vans and send 'em out. I could do it with a push of a button, but I'll be in the driver's seat for sure. But headed where I don't know or when I'll get there." He reaches for his cane wedged between the door and his seat. "Or how long any of it will take until I can stop." He taps his cane on his window. "I need out for a sec."

"What's wrong?"

"I just need out."

Shoshanna flicks on the hazards and coasts to the roadside. Clarence assists his legs out, wobbles, faces more than half a field cut down by a tractor guzzling along the horizon where dirt and seeds spiral. Bugs snap by; humidity fogs Clarence's glasses. The sounds of cutting blades circle back to him. A swelling heads his way and balloons his chest and sinuses—not summer heat but time growing large and telling him something he has to be small to hear; to neither listen nor speak; to not beg standing before it but to find direction.

He straggles back to the car. "I ran into Dennis Stohup the other day. I made a buggy for his daughter a long time ago. He wants me to make one for his grandkids."

"Are you?"

"I am." He taps his cane on the steering wheel. "I want to take us on a detour home."

"What about your break?"

"I had it."

As Shoshanna moves to the passenger seat, the boys wake up, and Clarence finds the oldies radio station. He turns his cane into a microphone, turns to the boys and Shoshanna, and drops snappy bass notes. He accelerates on the freeway looping around town, past the exit for the street with Tysons, into the other end of the county, and down a road spotted with horse stables and fences and a house with a long stone walkway to the front door where he knocks and steps back.

A wrinkled little woman in a yellow dress answers the door. "May I help you?"

"Mrs. Stohup?"

"Yes."

"My name's Clarence DeWare, and I built a buggy for your daughter when she was young."

"Yes, I remember."

"I talked to your husband the other day about making something for your grandkids."

"That would be wonderful for you to do for them."

"I was out running some errands in your neck of the woods, and I thought I'd stop by to see if he wanted to talk."

"That's so kind of you, but he's out right now."

Clarence leans on his cane. "When will he be back?"

"Can you talk tomorrow?"

"I sure can."

"After three work for you?"

"That's perfect," he says. "We see our daughter and son-in-law every Sunday. I'll stop by after that."

. . .

They return from church and the gravesite before noon; the boys mimic their growling stomachs as the car crosses hills leading home and turns for the driveway by the kitchen. Benjamin challenges Shaw they can wash their hands faster than last week: "I can time us, and we can beat it." But Clarence reminds them about changing from their good clothes into work clothes before washing their hands, and before lunch, because he needs their help loading samples into his pickup.

"But we'll literally die if we don't eat." Shaw's head wobbles side to side.

"I can't help you much, if my tummy is running on empty," Benjamin says. "My muscles will be like jelly."

After Clarence and Shoshanna glance at each other, Clarence says, "Benjy, I've got that drawerful of snacks."

He lights up. "The one with chocolate pieces?"

"Unless you ate it all."

"I haven't. I swear."

"And I may have snuck out a blueberry muffin from the other day."

"That's where it went." Shaw smacks his forehead. "I counted all of them but one."

"You two can split it."

"But we're not putting any butter on it if you have some out there. It's probably moldy."

The boys choke their necks and fake suffocation.

Clarence unlocks the back door. "Just because something's old doesn't mean you have to throw it out. You can repurpose it. Put it to better use."

"You can make penicillin from it."

Clarence beams at Shaw. "We can sell it." He spreads an imaginary sign across his pickup. "DeWare's Medicinal Mold. Available wherever fine mold is sold."

Shoshanna shakes her head, warms the oven, and listens to messages on the phone.

"Go change." Clarence loosens his tie and drapes his suit coat over a chair. "And meet me in the workshop in fifteen minutes." After the boys zip upstairs and the ceiling thunders, he digs at the back of the refrigerator for the wrapped blueberry muffin he hid. "I gotta plant this out there before they show up."

Shoshanna lowers the phone. "You got a message."

"Tysons calling me back in?" He nibbles the muffin before resealing it. "Surf's up, dude."

"Stohup changed his mind."

Clarence chokes for a second; his neck simmers. "What?"

"He wants to come here. Bring his grandkids. Not you going there. He'll be out and about." She kisses his cheek. "Like we were yesterday."

Clarence double-taps his cane on the floor before heading upstairs to the master bedroom and stopping by the boys' room. "Go ahead and change but wash up. We'll eat first then work. Pork chops and sweet potatoes."

The boys cheer.

After lunch and an hour of reading, Clarence starts the coffee pot on his workshop desk, powers on the computer, and reviews Stohup's folder and the old plans and notes from the buggy he made. He calculates in the margins and deletes, scribbles out, remeasures, and adds components based on what Stohup told him: smaller, no horse needed, stationary. Too small, Clarence mulls, and the result will be a toy, not something for children to play on and pretend they're going somewhere. Too large and it will need reins; working brakes, axles, tires; and a horse pulling it through the world.

"Grandad, he's here!" the boys yell, chasing each other into the workshop.

An SUV idles outside the big doors.

"Good to see you again." Stohup's boots crunch the ground. "Sorry I missed you yesterday."

"No problem at all."

The two men shake hands and pat their shoulders.

"These are my grandsons Benjamin and Shaw. My wife Shoshanna is taking a nap."

"Great day for a long nap. A lil' hot, but if you find some shade, the heat'll knock you out for hours."

"She's planning on that."

"Nice to meet you two young men." Stohup leans toward the boys. "Dennis."

Shaw blushes; Benjamin salutes.

"I'm not military. Just someone your grandaddy knows. He's gonna help us. Make us something."

The boys wave to two pairs of eyes peering from behind the SUV's window.

Stohup steps into the workshop. "Great to see behind the curtains."

"After I'm cold in the ground, it will still be a mess."

"I hear you." Stohup wipes his white beard. "Let me get Callie and Gordon." After he turns off the engine, he opens the rear-passenger door, pushes a button that, with a motorized hum, angles the chassis toward the ground, and helps his grandkids out —the boy and girl wearing compression socks and arm sleeves; the girl with a helmet and large glasses strapped under her forehead's scar.

Shaw and Benjamin run over and say hi to Gordon cowering behind Stohup who rubs his back and coaxes him with "They're gonna make that toy for you and Callie that Grandma and I talked about. Like your mom's."

"We sure are." Clarence rubs Gordon's head. "We'll make it like your mom's." He winks at Stohup. "What colors would you like?"

Gordon shies a little more.

"That's OK. You think about it. It's a big decision. We got all kinds of time for you to tell me. Maybe we can paint half one color for you and another color for your sister."

Gordon steps toward Shaw and Benjamin—Shaw taking his hand; Benjamin rambling on about so much in the workshop to play with but only after they work unless "Grandad excuses us to play first. But come on! Let's go!" Gordon cries; Shaw and Benjamin comfort him. Callie takes her time reaching them after Clarence, leaning on his cane, greets her and, tapping his gray temple, takes note of her favorite colors she tells him about. Gordon motions for her, and the kids continue deeper through shadows and light and fabric blowing over pieces of wood lined up to be shaped and filled.

ACKNOWLEDGMENTS

Thanks to the following publications where versions of stories in *Inroads* first appeared:

"Dioramas," *Tupelo Quarterly*

"Creek on the Right," *The Dead Mule School of Southern Literature*

"Moonflowers," *Illuminations*

To everyone who reads and supports me and my work—thank you.

And to H.

ABOUT THE AUTHOR

William Auten is the author of the novels *October*, *In Another Sun*, and *Pepper's Ghost* and the short-story collection *A Fine Day Will Burn Through*. williamauten.com